THE SECRETS OF VESUVIUS

Caroline Lawrence is American. She grew up in California and came to England when she won a scholarship to Cambridge to study Classical Archaeology, which she followed with a degree in Hebrew and Jewish studies at the University of London. She lives by the river in London with her husband, a graphic designer.

To find out more about the Roman Mysteries visit www.romanmysteries.com

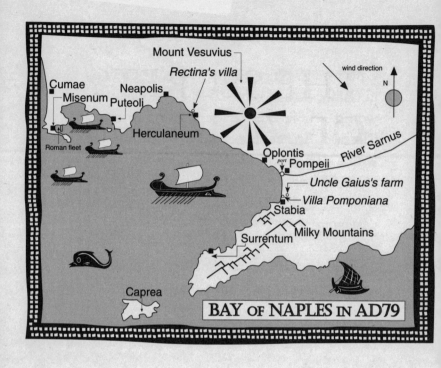

Mount Vesuvius

Rectina's villa

wind direction

N

Cumae
Misenum
Neapolis
Puteoli

Herculaneum

Roman fleet

Oplontis
port
Pompeii

River Sarnus

Uncle Gaius's farm

Villa Pomponiana

Stabia

Milky Mountains

Surrentum

Caprea

BAY OF NAPLES IN AD79

A Roman Mystery

THE SECRETS
OF VESUVIUS

Caroline Lawrence

Orion
Children's Books

First published in Great Britain in 2001
by Orion Children's Books
This paperback edition published 2002 by Dolphin
a division of the Orion Publishing Group Ltd
Orion House
5 Upper St Martin's Lane
London WC2H 9EA

10

A catalogue record for this book is
available from the British Library

ISBN-10 1 84255 021 7
ISBN-13 978 1 84255 021 2

Typeset at The Spartan Press Ltd,
Lymington, Hants

Printed and bound in Great Britain by
Clays Ltd, St Ives plc

www.orionbooks.co.uk <http://www.orionbooks.co.uk/>

*To all my students
past, present and future*

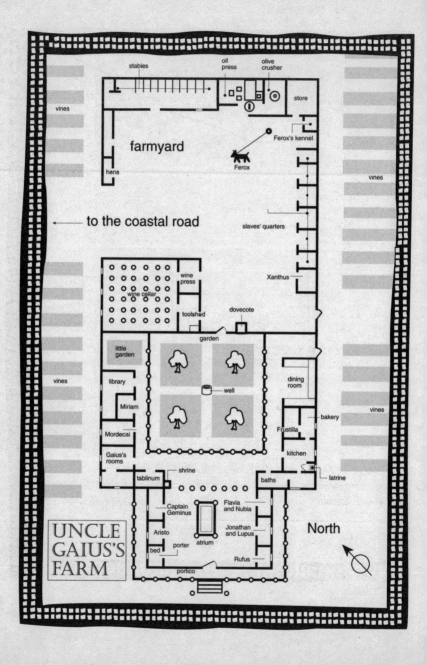

UNCLE GAIUS'S FARM

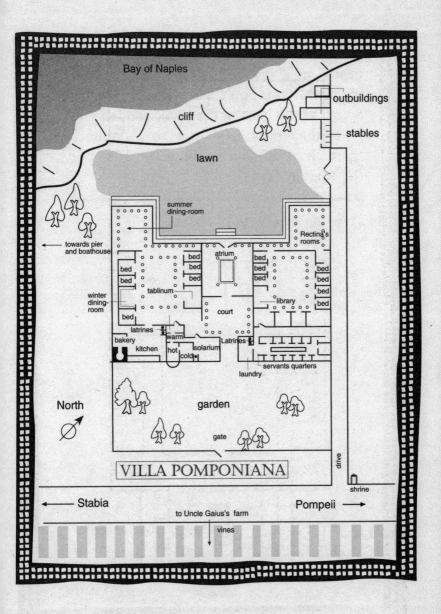

Bay of Naples

outbuildings

stables

cliff

lawn

summer
dining-room

towards pier
and boathouse

Recina's
rooms

bed

atrium

bed

bed

bed

bed

bed

bed

bed

bed

bed

bed

bed

tablinum

bed

library

bed

winter
dining-
room

court

bed

latrines

warm

Latrines

bakery

kitchen

hot

cold

solarium

laundry

servants quarters

North

garden

gate

VILLA POMPONIANA

drive

shrine

Stabia

Pompeii

to Uncle Gaius's farm

vines

This story takes place in Ancient Roman times, so a few of the words may look strange. If you don't know them, 'Aristo's Scroll' at the back of the book will tell you what they mean and how to pronounce them. It also explains about the hours of the Roman day.

SCROLL I

'Jonathan, look out!' screamed Flavia Gemina.

Jonathan ben Mordecai – hip deep in the blue Tyrrhenian sea – didn't see the horrible creature rising out of the water behind him.

'Arrrgh!' The sea monster seized Jonathan round the waist.

'Aiieeee!' cried Jonathan. But his scream was cut off as he was pulled under, and salt water filled his mouth and nostrils. A moment later the surface of the water sparkled peacefully under the hot summer sun. Flavia and her slave-girl Nubia stared in horror.

Suddenly Jonathan shot up again in an explosion of spray and foam, gasping for air. He spat out a mouthful of seawater.

'Lupus, you fool, I could have drowned!'

Another figure popped up out of the water beside him, laughing hard. It was Lupus the sea monster, naked as an eel. Although Lupus was only eight years old, Flavia squealed at the sight of his nakedness and shut her eyes. She heard Lupus splash through the waves onto the beach.

When she thought it was safe to look, Flavia opened one eye.

Lupus was tying the cord belt of his tunic.

Flavia opened the other eye.

Jonathan was creeping up behind Lupus with a large scoop of wet sand in one hand. Before he could drop the sand down the back of Lupus's tunic, the younger boy spun round and tackled Jonathan. They fell onto the sand, where they rolled around like a pair of wrestlers in the palaestra.

Finally Jonathan, who was older and bigger, ended up on top. He straddled Lupus's waist and held the younger boy's wrists hard against the hot sand. Lupus struggled and strained, but although he was strong and wiry, he couldn't budge Jonathan.

'Ha!' crowed Jonathan. 'The warrior Achilles has overpowered the fierce sea monster. Beg for mercy. Go on. Say *pax*!'

Flavia sighed and rolled her eyes.

'Jonathan, you *know* Lupus can't speak. He doesn't have a tongue. How can he beg for mercy? Let him go.'

'No,' insisted Jonathan. 'No mercy until he begs for it. Do you want mercy?'

Lupus's green eyes blazed. He shook his head defiantly as he tried to struggle free.

'Then you will receive the punishment!' Jonathan let a glob of foamy saliva emerge from his mouth. It hung over Lupus's face.

Lupus looked up in alarm at the dangling spit. Flavia and Nubia squealed. Suddenly a furry wet creature hurled itself at Jonathan, barking enthusiastically.

'Scuto!' laughed Jonathan. He fell off Lupus as the dog covered his face with hot kisses. Two wet puppies scrambled after the bigger dog.

Scuto waited until the four friends had gathered around him. Then he shook himself vigorously. The puppies followed suit, shaking their small bodies from head to tail.

'*En!*' said Nubia. 'Behold! My new tunic is bespattered.'

Jonathan laughed. 'I think we've been reading you too much Latin poetry.'

Flavia looked down at her own tunic, which was also spotted with salt water. 'Oh well, only one thing to do . . .'

She ran squealing into the water, tunic and all. The other three yelled and followed her.

For several minutes they splashed and dunked each other. Then Lupus gave the older children their daily swimming lesson. He showed them how to move through the water by pulling with their arms and making their legs move like a frog's. Nubia, who had grown up in the African desert, where water was rare and precious, had been shy of the sea at first. Now she loved swimming. Jonathan was making good progress, too. But Flavia couldn't get her arms and legs to work together.

At last they all emerged from the sea and fell in a row onto the soft, warm dunes. Breathing hard, the four of them closed their eyes and let the hot August sun dry them. The sea breeze was deliciously cool against their wet bodies. Scuto and the puppies, Nipur and Tigris, lay panting on the sand.

When she'd caught her breath, Flavia lifted herself on one elbow and squinted up the beach. Sextus, one of her father's sailors, lay dozing under a papyrus parasol meant for the two girls.

Having their own private bodyguard was more than a luxury. Only a few weeks earlier, Flavia and her friends had narrowly escaped capture by Venalicius the slave-dealer. If he had caught them, he could have taken them anywhere in the Mediterranean and sold them as slaves, never to be found again. But Sextus was nearby, and for the moment they were safe.

Flavia lay back on the warm sand and gazed up at a seagull drifting in the pure blue expanse of the sky. She could taste the salt on her lips and hear the whisper of waves on the wet sand. Her friends lay beside her and the dogs dozed at her feet.

Flavia Gemina closed her eyes and sighed. She wished every day could be like this. But her father had decided that Ostia was not a safe place for them to spend the rest of the summer. In two days they would sail south to her uncle's farm near Pompeii.

That was a pity. The farm was safe. But dull.

Flavia sighed again.

She had enjoyed her first taste of detective work, when she and her friends had discovered and trapped Ostia's dog-killer. She wanted more mysteries to solve. And there were plenty here in Ostia. A nine-year-old girl named Sapphira had gone missing a few months earlier. Alma's favourite baker had been robbed three times. And there were always mysterious strangers lurking near the harbour, hoping to catch a fast boat away from Italy. Living in a busy seaport like Ostia, you needed to use all your senses and be constantly on the alert.

'What is it, Jonathan?' said Flavia. 'Why do you keep poking me?'

'You were snoring,' he said. 'And I think someone's in trouble.'

Flavia sat up and shaded her eyes with her hand.

Far out on the vast expanse of glittering blue water, she could just make out the curve of an upturned rowing boat. And clinging to it was a tiny figure frantically waving for help!

SCROLL II

The four friends scrambled to their feet and gazed out to sea.

'Behold. A sturdy vessel has capsized!' said Nubia.

'Sextus!' cried Flavia. 'Quick!'

The big bodyguard scrambled to his feet and looked around in alarm.

'A boat's capsized!' she yelled.

The three dogs barked and bounced round the sailor as he ran up to them. He was tanned and muscular, and would have been good-looking if most of his teeth hadn't been missing.

'What?' he said, and then, 'Where?'

They all pointed.

It took Sextus only a moment to assess the situation. Cursing under his breath, he stripped off his tunic, ran splashing through the shallow water and then swam towards the upturned boat with strong, powerful strokes.

Lupus ran to the water's edge, hesitated, then took off his own tunic.

'Lupus, no! It's too far,' they cried.

Lupus ignored their shouts. He plunged into the water and began to swim after Sextus.

To Flavia, it seemed ages before Sextus reached the upturned boat. She breathed a sigh of relief as Lupus's smaller head finally joined the other two. But instead of swimming back at once, the three figures stayed with the boat, bobbing up and down.

'What are they doing?' said Jonathan.

Finally the two larger heads began moving back towards the beach. After a moment the smaller head followed, but more slowly than before.

Nubia gripped Flavia's arm anxiously. 'Lupus getting tired.'

'You're right,' said Flavia. 'He'll be exhausted.'

'I have an idea,' said Jonathan. 'I'll run to the marina and hire a litter to carry them home. Father can treat them.'

'Good idea,' said Flavia. 'But what about your asthma? I'd better go. I can run faster.' When she saw the expression on his face she gave his shoulder a quick squeeze. 'You stay and protect Nubia. Scuto will protect me.'

Flavia's bare feet slapped against the wet sand – she had left her sandals on the dunes. Never mind, no time to go back now. Scuto ran beside her, his tongue lolling. Soon she could see the marina where fishing boats and smaller merchant ships were docked.

Her heart was beating fast as she and Scuto ran over

the softer dunes, past the synagogue and up towards the quay. A boardwalk separated the marina on the left from warehouses and temples on the right. As Flavia ran past the piers she looked to see if the slave-ship Vespa was moored there. Thankfully, its hateful yellow and black sail was nowhere in sight. Venalicius and his crew must be on their way to Delos, or one of the other slave-trading centres.

The area around the Marina Gate was crowded. Flavia hooked her finger through Scuto's collar as she dodged sailors, shoppers, soldiers and slaves. She needed a litter, and she needed one quickly. There were usually one or two under the arch of the gate. They offered lifts around Ostia for a few sestercii.

She kept her left hand tightly over her money pouch. In this crush, thieves would be everywhere.

At last she spotted a litter in a patch of shade near the Marina Gate. Beside it lounged two muscular young men eating their lunch: greasy pieces of meat on wooden skewers.

'How much . . . to hire your litter . . . for half an hour?' She stood breathlessly in front of them.

'What, darling? Want a ride, do you?' grinned one of the litter-bearers. His ears were shaped like broccoli.

'Capsized boat,' Flavia gasped. 'My friends are rescuing him. How much to carry him . . . to a house near the Laurentum Gate?' She jingled her coin purse urgently.

'Four sestercii, sweetheart,' said the other one, whose nose was not unlike a turnip. 'I'm giving you a special rate because it's a good deed we're doing.'

'And because it's been slow all morning,' grumbled Broccoli-ears under his breath, and tossed the last greasy gob of meat to Scuto.

Flavia and her hired litter-bearers were about a hundred yards up the beach when she saw Sextus stagger out of the water and onto the shore, half pulling and half carrying a portly man.

Barking loudly, Scuto raced ahead towards the group on the shore. As the dog approached, the stout man abruptly sat down on the sand. Scuto, his tail wagging vigorously, licked the man's face and then hurried on to greet the others.

'You're just in time,' cried Jonathan, running to meet Flavia and the litter. 'His lips are turning blue. We need to wrap him in a blanket and get him to my father as quickly as possible.'

Broccoli-ears and Turnip-nose knew their job. They lifted the man and helped him into the litter. He was stout and tanned, with a fringe of white hair round his bald head. And he was wheezing, the way Jonathan sometimes did. As Flavia helped the litter-bearers tuck a faded green blanket around him, she noticed a heavy gold ring on his finger.

'Do you want the curtains open or shut, darling?' asked Turnip-nose.

9

'Open,' said Flavia. 'So we can see how he's doing.'

'Wait,' gasped the man. It was the first time he had spoken. 'Where is my bag?' His voice was high and breathy.

'He insisted we take it,' explained Sextus, coming up to the litter. 'Lupus has it.'

Flavia turned to see Nubia helping Lupus out of the sea. The boy staggered across the sand to the litter and held out a dripping oilcloth bag. The man, now comfortably propped up on his cushions, grasped it eagerly.

'Thank you, thank you,' he cried in his light voice. 'This is all that matters.' He reached into the bag and they all waited to see what priceless treasure he would pull out of it.

It was a wax tablet and stylus. The man grunted with satisfaction, opened the tablet and shook drops of water from it. Then he began to write. They all stared at him. After a moment he looked back at them.

'Well, why are we waiting?' he wheezed cheerfully. 'Off you go, bearers, to wherever you are taking me.'

'Wait!' cried Flavia. 'I know who you are!'

SCROLL III

'You're Pliny, aren't you?' said Flavia. 'The man who wrote the *Natural History*.'

'Why, yes. Yes, I am,' said the man in the litter. 'How did you know that?'

'Well –' began Flavia, and then caught sight of Lupus, dripping and shivering. 'Please may Lupus share your litter?'

'Of course, of course!' Pliny gestured to the litter-bearers.

Broccoli-ears and Turnip-nose helped the exhausted boy climb up onto the other end of the couch. They settled him against a cushion facing Pliny. Then Broccoli-ears took the two poles at the front of the litter and Turnip-nose took those at the rear. When the strong young men had adjusted the balance, they set off back up the beach.

'Tell me how you guessed my identity.' Pliny closed his wax tablet and looked at Flavia.

'Well,' she began, jogging a little to keep up. 'You sat on the sand when Scuto ran up to you. In volume eight you say that the best way to calm an attacking dog is to sit on the ground.'

'You've read volume eight of my book?'

'Yes, I have the whole set,' admitted Flavia with a shy laugh. 'It's a pleasure to meet you, sir. My name is Flavia Gemina, daughter of Marcus Flavius Geminus, sea captain.'

'It's a pleasure to meet you, too, Flavia Gemina,' said Pliny. 'But I am not the only person who sits down when a fierce dog approaches. You must have had other clues . . .'

'I did. I know the author of the *Natural History* is an admiral who lives just down the coast. Your face is tanned as if you've spent time in the sun, but your hands are soft and ink-stained, like the hands of a scholar. I can tell from your ring that you're rich and high-born.' Flavia took a breath and carried on.

'I also heard that a killer whale was spotted in the harbour yesterday. You wrote a book about natural history. So that would explain why you were out in a small boat with your tablet and stylus.' Most of this was occurring to Flavia as she spoke, but the old man's shining eyes encouraged her.

'Furthermore,' she proclaimed dramatically, 'I think the killer whale surfaced near your boat and . . . and capsized it with his tail.'

'Extraordinary!' cried Pliny, clapping his hands. 'What a superb mind you have for deductions. However, I am afraid you are incorrect about the cause of my accident. We never saw the killer whale. Rather, my stupid slave panicked when a wasp flew too near. He stood up and flapped his arms about, with the inevitable results. I'm afraid he has paid dearly for his fear of being stung. I shouldn't have taken a mere household slave.'

'You mean your slave is dead?' gulped Jonathan, jogging on the other side of the litter.

'Yes, indeed. I'm afraid he now lies at the bottom of the Tyrrhenian Sea. But who are you, young man, and where are you taking me?'

'I'm Jonathan ben Mordecai. My father is a doctor. He'll help you recover.'

'Ah!' said the admiral. 'A Jew! Jews make extraordinarily good doctors. I look forward to meeting him. However, I don't think there is anything wrong with me that a cup of wine and a piece of cheese won't cure. I've been floating in that water since two hours past dawn. I'm as wrinkled as a raisin and ravenously hungry.'

'I'm sure my father has some wine,' said Jonathan, and then added, 'I've read some of your book, too.'

'How gratifying! I am surrounded by fans. Do you also enjoy my writings, young lady?' This last was addressed to Nubia, who smiled shyly and then looked rather frightened.

'Nubia has only been here in Italy for two months,' Flavia explained, 'She's learning to speak Latin but can't read it yet.'

'And you, young man, the brave and aquatic hero

who rescued my precious tablets and notes. What is your name?'

'His name is Lupus,' answered Jonathan. 'He is an orphan and can't speak. His tongue was cut out.'

'Poor boy!' said Pliny, 'How did it happen?'

Lupus's grin instantly faded and his green eyes stared coldly into the admiral's. Pliny's cheerful gaze faltered and he looked uncertainly at Flavia.

'We don't know how Lupus lost his tongue,' she whispered. 'He lives with Jonathan now, and has lessons with us. We hope one day he'll be able to tell us in writing. But he doesn't like people talking about it.'

They had just passed through the cool shade of the Marina Gate. Now the litter emerged into the bright, hot sunshine and turned right onto Marina Street, just inside the city walls. Although many people were making their way home or to taverns in order to eat the midday meal, it was still crowded.

Lupus's face brightened again and he beamed around at the lesser mortals who had to walk on foot. Suddenly he startled them all by crowing like a rooster at two scruffy boys loitering in front of a snack bar. The boys saw him and whooped back.

'Lupus in a litter!' cried one of them.

'Are you rich, now?' yelled the other.

Lupus nodded smugly and stuck his nose in the air in a parody of a rich man. One of the boys picked up a rotten lettuce from the gutter and threw it at the litter. The soggy green missile struck Jonathan on the back.

'Hey!' Jonathan turned around, but the boys had darted out of sight.

'Perhaps we should close the curtains now,' Pliny said to Flavia.

Lupus clutched Pliny's ankle and shook his head imploringly.

'Very well,' said Pliny. 'But if you ride in a litter you must behave with decorum and not bellow out at your comrades.'

Lupus nodded meekly and behaved himself for the rest of the journey home.

'Well, that was delicious,' said Pliny, patting his ample stomach. 'I owe you all a great debt – you saved my life. But even more importantly, you fed me. I hate missing my midday meal.'

They were all in the cool triclinium of Flavia's house: the adults reclining on couches against the wall, Flavia and her friends sitting round a table in the centre. The dining-room opened out onto a bright inner garden with a fig tree, fountain and scented shrubs.

Reclining on Pliny's right was Flavia's father. Marcus Flavius Geminus was tall and tanned, with light brown hair and the same clear grey eyes as his daughter. His hand trembled nervously as he refilled the admiral's wine cup. He could scarcely believe he was entertaining the Commander-in-Chief of the Roman imperial fleet.

Admiral Pliny nodded his thanks and then turned to Jonathan's father Mordecai, who reclined on his left.

'Thank you for looking after me, doctor.'

'It was nothing.' Mordecai bowed his turbaned head. 'I merely prescribed mint tea and a light lunch to revive you.'

'And it has. Particularly this delightful wine.' Pliny lifted his cup towards Captain Geminus. 'Is it from the Vesuvius region?'

'Why, yes.' Flavia's father looked impressed. 'My brother Gaius has an estate near Pompeii. This wine is from his vineyards.'

'I know the region well. In fact, I am going down to Misenum in less than a week, as soon as the festivals have finished.' Pliny folded his napkin and smiled at them all. 'And now, much as I'd like to stay and chat, I must be getting back. My household will begin to worry and I am a busy man. However, I would like to invite you four children to dine with me at my Laurentum villa tomorrow evening. Will you come?'

'We'd love to come,' Flavia said, flushing with pleasure.

'Excellent,' said the admiral. 'I'll send my carriage for you at the ninth hour. You see, I've already thanked your bodyguard for rescuing me, but I'd like to give each of you a small reward, too.'

SCROLL IV

The following afternoon, soon after the four friends returned from the baths, a two-horse carruca pulled up outside Flavia's house.

It was only a few miles from Ostia to Laurentum, a pleasant drive along the coastal road. The carriage crunched up the gravel drive of Pliny's seaside villa less than half an hour after they had left Ostia. A door-slave in a red tunic met them on the steps of the butter-coloured villa and led them through cool rooms and sunny courtyards to a breezy dining-room.

Flavia and her friends gazed around in amazement.

The room they stood in was surrounded on three sides by water. Only a low wall and spiral columns separated them from the blue Mediterranean. Jonathan and Lupus immediately went to the marble parapet and leaned over.

'Careful!' wheezed Admiral Pliny, shuffling into the room. 'We're right above the sea.'

'*Salve!*' they all said, and he returned their greeting.

'These halls are fair,' said Nubia.

'It is a rather fine triclinium, isn't it?' Pliny was

wearing a faded purple tunic and leather slippers. He held a wax tablet in one hand. 'When the wind's from the south-west you can actually feel the spray from the breakers.'

'And look at that view!' Flavia pointed back the way they had just come. A slave had opened the double front doors and they could see all the way back through the house to the gravel drive and green woods beyond.

'It's the most beautiful villa I've ever seen,' said Jonathan.

Lupus nodded vigorously.

Pliny smiled.

'My only complaint,' he said, 'is that there is no aqueduct to supply us with running water. It makes a bit more work for the bath-slaves. But there are several wells and springs on the property.'

'You have your own private baths?' Jonathan's jaw dropped.

'Oh yes. Steam room, cold plunge, heated swimming pool . . . I simply can't do without my bath.'

A handsome slave in a red tunic hurried into the room. Around his neck hung a scribe's inkpot on a chain.

'Ah, Phrixus! Just in time.'

Admiral Pliny turned to Flavia and her friends.

'Please be seated.' He gestured towards a table set with five places. 'I prefer to sit for my meals rather than recline. I usually have a slave read to me while I eat and it's easier to take notes sitting down.'

Two female slaves in blue entered the sunny dining-room on bare feet, holding silver basins and linen napkins to wash the diners' hands. Nearby, in the shadow of a column, a fair-haired boy in a red tunic played soft music on pan pipes.

The food was simple but delicious: hardboiled eggs to start, chicken and salad for the main course and sweet red apples for dessert. The two serving-girls kept the cups filled with well-watered wine and passed out rolls made from the finest white flour.

As they ate, Pliny told them amusing stories about the Emperor Vespasian, who had been his friend. Occasionally the admiral turned to his scribe and dictated a few lines. The young slave had smooth, tanned skin and dark curly hair. He reminded Flavia of her tutor, though Aristo's hair was lighter.

Finally, as they munched slices of apple, Pliny leaned back in his chair.

'Now, Flavia Gemina, I believe you recently solved the mystery of Ostia's dog-killer!'

'You know about that?' Flavia felt her face grow pink.

'Of course. Research is what I do best.' The admiral's eyes twinkled, and he added, 'I know Ostia's junior magistrate fairly well. He was very impressed with your detective work. Tell me how you did it.'

A sea breeze ruffled their hair and garments.

'Well, I couldn't have done it without my friends.'

For the first time that evening, Pliny ignored his Greek scribe and gave them his undivided attention. His eyes shone as Flavia and Jonathan took it in turns to tell the story. He laughed at Lupus's sound-effects and when, after much coaxing, Nubia shyly sang her haunting Dog-Song, the admiral wiped a tear from his eye.

'Extraordinary,' said Pliny. 'You are quite remarkable children.'

He glanced at his scribe and Flavia thought he was going to resume his dictation. Instead, the young man slipped out of the dining-room and returned a moment later with three small pouches and a papyrus scroll.

'Thank you, Phrixus.' Pliny looked around the table at each of them. 'I promised you all a reward for rescuing me yesterday and I hope my modest gifts will not disappoint you.

'First, to Lupus, the brave young swimmer who rescued my precious research . . .' Pliny nodded at Phrixus, who presented Lupus with a small, blue silk pouch.

Lupus opened it with eager hands and tipped out the contents. A gold ring set with an engraved aquamarine fell into his palm.

'What is it?' Flavia asked.

'It is a signet ring with a wolf carved upon it,' said the admiral. 'Most suitable for someone whose name means "wolf".'

Lupus passed it around. They all admired the miniature wolf's face cut into the gem. Lupus looked at Pliny with bright eyes and nodded his head respectfully.

'You're most welcome,' said Pliny in his breathy voice. 'Next, the dusky Nubia. Unwillingly taken from your desert home, you bravely face the future as a stranger in a strange land.'

Phrixus presented Nubia with a tiny pouch of orange silk. Inside were two earrings: golden brown gems in gold settings.

'The stone is called "tiger's-eye",' explained the admiral, 'because the yellow streak looks like a cat's eye.'

'Thank you, sir,' said Nubia, putting in the earrings. They gleamed in her neat ears, perfectly matching the colour of her eyes.

'Jonathan,' continued Pliny, 'I understand you suffer from asthma, as I do.'

Phrixus handed Jonathan a small leather pouch on a black silken cord.

'In this pouch are exotic and rare herbs for your shortness of breath. Such a bag of herbs has brought me relief on many occasions. Always wear it round your neck. When you feel the tightening in your chest, breathe into it.'

'Thank you, admiral,' said Jonathan. He gave the sack a tentative sniff.

'And finally, a gift for you, my dear.' Pliny smiled at

Flavia. 'Something which I hope will appeal to your enquiring mind.'

Phrixus handed Flavia a papyrus scroll, tied with a blue ribbon. As she untied the ribbon, Pliny explained,

'It's an unpublished work of mine, written in my own hand when I was younger. It's a short account of some of the great mysteries of the past. I meant to include it as an appendix to my book *The Scholar*, but in the end I left it out.'

Wide-eyed, Flavia unrolled the scroll carefully. Minuscule writing covered the sheet from margin to margin.

'Thank you,' breathed Flavia. 'I love mysteries.'

The admiral nodded. Then he narrowed his eyes and stroked his chin thoughtfully.

'I think I might have a real mystery for you to solve. You say you are travelling to the Pompeii region soon?'

'Yes,' replied Flavia. 'My uncle Gaius lives between Stabia and Pompeii.'

'Perfect!' exclaimed the admiral. 'Phrixus, do you have –' but the Greek scribe was already holding out a scrap of papyrus.

'What a marvellous servant you are, Phrixus,' said Pliny with a smile. 'You anticipate my every wish. Please give it to our young detective.'

Flavia eagerly took the piece of papyrus and read it. Then she looked up at Pliny, a frown creasing her forehead.

'It's only a riddle,' she said. 'A child's riddle.'

'Yes,' said Pliny, 'but it may lead you to a great treasure!'

SCROLL V

'Read us the riddle,' said Jonathan, leaning forward in his chair.

'*Littera prima dolet, secunda iubet, tertia mittit, quarta docet, et littera quinta gaudet,*' read Flavia. 'My first letter grieves, my second commands, my third sends, my fourth teaches, and my fifth letter rejoices.' Flavia frowned at the piece of papyrus.

'I know this kind of puzzle!' cried Jonathan. 'When you guess all the letters, they spell out a word. And I think I know what the first letter is. "My first letter grieves" means the letter *A*, pronounced "ah!", because that's the sound you make when you're sad. May I see it?'

'Do *you* know the answer, Admiral Pliny?' asked Flavia, handing Jonathan the papyrus.

The admiral shook his head. 'I'm afraid I don't. The riddle is a bit of graffiti I saw about a month ago, on the wall of a blacksmith's workshop in Pompeii. The young smith who repaired my cart-wheel saw me studying the riddle. He assured me that the answer would lead me to a most valuable treasure. "A treasure beyond imagining" were his precise words.'

Pliny took the papyrus scrap from Jonathan and studied it thoughtfully.

'I should very much like to know the answer to the riddle,' he said, 'because I believe it is genuine. There was something special about the blacksmith . . . I went back the following week to speak to him, but he wasn't there. If you should find him, or solve the riddle, send a messenger to me at this address in Misenum. I'm going down after the festival of Jove.' The admiral handed the riddle to Phrixus, who dipped his pen in the hanging inkpot and wrote the address on the back.

'So you see,' said the admiral, blowing on the ink and flapping the papyrus, 'this is a two-part mystery. Solve the riddle. And find the blacksmith.'

'Do you happen to know –' began Jonathan.

'The blacksmith's name?' Pliny rose smiling from his chair. 'I do indeed – it is Vulcan, a most suitable name for a blacksmith.'

'Vulcan?' said Nubia.

'The god of blacksmiths and metalworkers,' said Flavia. 'Vulcan!'

Two days later, Flavia and Jonathan lay on their backs on a sun-warmed ship's deck, gazing up at the blue sky and the taut canvas sail. Beneath them, the merchant ship *Myrtilla* rose and fell, almost like a living creature.

A strong breeze had filled the ship's sail and for two days the *Myrtilla* had ploughed a creamy path through the sapphire sea. On the previous evening, the *Myrtilla* had anchored in a cove and they had spent the night sleeping on a crescent beach under a million stars.

There were seven passengers on board: Flavia and her three friends, plus Jonathan's father Mordecai and sister Miriam, and Flavia's young Greek tutor Aristo. Flavia's father, the owner and captain of the ship, sat at the helm with the steering paddle in his right hand. Occasionally he barked a command to his four crew members, the Phoenician brothers Quartus, Quintus and Sextus, and an Ethiopian named Ebenus.

'Nubia seems to have got over her fear of ships,' Jonathan observed.

Flavia's slave-girl was high in the rigging with Lupus. Earlier in the day, the two of them had seen one of the Phoenician brothers go up and had followed him like monkeys. Now Nubia was playing her lotus-wood flute while Lupus drummed a beat on the oak mast. Their music seemed to fill the sail and carry the ship forward.

Mordecai and Aristo sat chatting in the shade of the cabin, near Scuto and the puppies. For their own safety the dogs had been housed in a wooden cage with a straw-covered floor. They were not enjoying themselves and stared out resentfully at their owners. Miriam stood alone at the front of the ship. The wind whipped her curly dark hair and violet mantle as she leaned over the prow.

'Let's get back to Pliny's riddle,' said Flavia. 'You

say the first letter is *A*, the sound for sadness. But then what?' They had been trying to solve the puzzle since the evening of Pliny's dinner party.

'I was thinking about it last night on the beach,' said Jonathan. 'The sound for rejoicing might be the letter *E*, pronounced "eh!".' He punched the air, as if his favourite chariot team had just won.

'So it starts with the letter *A* and ends with *E*.' Flavia thoughtfully picked at one of the gummy ridges of pine pitch which sealed the planks of the deck.

'And I think "my third letter sends" means the letter *I*, because "*i!*" means "go!". If you tell someone to go, you send them away.'

'So it could be a word spelled *A*-something-*I*-something-*E*.' Flavia frowned. 'What's a Latin word that ends in *E*?'

'There are hundreds. Lots of words end in *E* when you are speaking to someone –'

'Or praying to one of the gods! Of course! Why didn't I think of that?' Flavia sat up so that she could think more clearly. 'So we only need letter two and letter four: "my second commands" and "my fourth teaches" –'

'*En!*' cried Nubia, high in the rigging. 'Behold!'

'She's right!' cried Flavia. '*En* means "behold" or "look". The riddle says "my fourth teaches": so *N* could fit, because in a way, it teaches. So we have *A-something-I-N-E . . .*'

'*En!*' cried Nubia again, more urgently: 'Behold!'

27

She was pointing back and to the left. Then Lupus pointed, too, and suddenly Quartus cried,

'To port, to port!'

'She's not giving us the next clue,' said Flavia, scrambling to her feet. 'She really wants to show us something!'

Flavia ran to the side of the ship and Jonathan followed, staggering a little as the deck rose and fell beneath him.

They leaned over the polished oak rail and gazed back.

A long, low warship was moving up quickly behind them. With its bristling oars and the eye painted on the prow, it reminded Flavia of some kind of dangerous insect.

'Like bug.' Nubia's voice from above echoed Flavia's thought.

The warship was already beside them, so close that they could see the water dripping from the flashing oars and hear the song of the oarsmen. The officer leading the chant was walking forward, so that he seemed to be overtaking the *Myrtilla* on foot. At the ship's stern a figure sat in the shade of the open cabin.

Flavia squinted. 'Maybe it's Pliny.'

'I don't think so.' Flavia's father joined them at the rail. 'The admiral said he was coming down tomorrow. But that ship is certainly one under his command, probably on manoeuvres from the naval harbour at Misenum.'

They waved as the warship slid past and the singing young officer grinned and waved back. The oarsmen were too intent on their rowing even to look at the ship they were overtaking. Soon the warship had pulled far ahead and disappeared behind a honey-coloured shoulder of rock.

'By Hercules, they're fast,' said Aristo.

'Superb!' agreed Mordecai.

'They have the benefit of eighty oarsmen as well as the wind full in their sail,' said Captain Geminus with a grin.

As they approached the promontory, the *Myrtilla*'s crew had one of its periodic bursts of activity when Captain Geminus bellowed and three of the crewmen swarmed over the rigging.

When the activity finally subsided, the *Myrtilla* had changed direction and was sailing into a vast blue bay.

'There it is,' said Flavia. 'The great bay of Neapolis.'

SCROLL VI

Jonathan had never seen so many boats in his entire life. Not even in the port of Ostia. They had passed the naval harbour of Misenum and the port of Puteoli on their left, and were now sailing towards a large mountain.

'That, of course, is Vesuvius,' said Flavia's father. 'It's covered with vineyards; which is why it's so green. You can see a few red roofs among the vines. Those are villas of the very rich.'

'How great and marvellous are your works,' murmured Mordecai. A breeze touched the two locks of grey hair which hung from his black turban. 'Truly this place is like paradise.'

'Pliny says this is the most fertile region in the whole world,' said Flavia.

'Does your uncle own one of those villas on the mountain?' Jonathan asked her.

'No,' said Flavia, 'he lives further south, between Pompeii and Stabia.'

'Where?'

Captain Geminus pointed again: 'See the town at the foot of Vesuvius?'

'Yes.'

'That's Herculaneum. Then . . . look right – no further – yes, there. That's Pompeii and then . . . do you see that small cluster of red roofs a bit further to the right? That's Stabia. My brother lives nearer to Stabia than Pompeii. But we'll disembark in Pompeii. The harbour at Stabia is murder to get in and out of.'

It was late afternoon by the time the *Myrtilla* sailed into the port of Pompeii. The vast blue bowl of the sky was filled with the piercing cries of swifts, which had begun to fly lower as the day cooled.

Pompeii was built on a hill, and they could see the imposing town walls across the water, orange in the rays of the sinking sun. The red roofs of the tallest buildings peeped above.

Using the large paddle at the back of the ship, Flavia's father guided the *Myrtilla* into the harbour. When the ship was moored, they all made their way carefully down the boarding plank.

'I must organise my berth with the harbourmaster,' said Captain Geminus, looking around. 'Ah, here he comes. Can you wait at that tavern over there across the square, the one with the yellow awning and plane trees? We'll bring the baggage and dogs over in a few minutes.'

The seven passengers made their way slowly past a forest of elegant masts. Coloured pennants fluttered and the tackle jingled musically in the late afternoon breeze. After two days on the springy wood of the *Myrtilla*'s deck, the pier felt hard and unyielding under Flavia's feet, and jarred her heels as she walked.

The harbour shrine of Castor and Pollux was wreathed with garlands, for it was the Ides of August, a day sacred to Jupiter, Diana and the Twins. The shops and taverns around the square were all clean and swept. Many had hanging baskets of violets and daisies.

Fresh from an afternoon at the baths and still dressed in their festive clothes, the young Pompeians strolled along the waterfront as the day cooled, perfumed girls in wisps of silk and young men in sea-green tunics with their hair slicked back. Some wore flowered garlands on their heads. Flavia wondered whether Vulcan the blacksmith was among them.

At the tavern with the yellow awning, Mordecai ordered two jugs of well-watered wine. The serving-girl brought the wine immediately and returned a few moments later with bowls of nuts.

'Mmmm, pistachio nuts!' said Jonathan, taking a handful. 'You don't get free nuts with your wine in Ostia.'

'That's because Pompeii is a much more elegant place than Ostia.' Aristo lifted his wine cup towards the city walls.

'And more expensive, too,' grumbled Mordecai, as he counted out coins for the girl.

'Here comes your father already,' Jonathan said to Flavia, spitting out a shell. Then he frowned: 'He's changed his clothes!'

Nubia frowned, too: 'He's had his hairs cut.'

'And it appears he's bought himself a new pair of boots, as well.' Mordecai tugged his beard in puzzlement.

Lupus grinned and shook his head, as if to say they were all mistaken.

'Uncle Gaius!' squealed Flavia. She jumped up from her chair, vaulted over a planter full of daisies and threw herself into her uncle's arms.

Gaius Flavius Geminus Senior was ten minutes older than his twin brother Marcus, who hurried up a few minutes later, followed by Quartus with the luggage and Sextus with the dogs.

'Gaius!' Flavia's father dropped the sea bag he was carrying and embraced his brother. 'You got my letter! I wasn't sure I'd sent it in time. I was going to take rooms in a tavern and organise a carriage tomorrow!'

'Your letter came yesterday. Xanthus has the cart ready and waiting, with a couple of horses tethered behind. If we go now we'll be home before dark.'

'But Uncle Gaius!' said Flavia. 'I wanted to spend the night in Pompeii. I wanted to look around the town. There's someone here I want to find.'

'Don't be silly.' Her uncle ruffled her already tousled hair. 'We're expecting you at the farm. You can see Pompeii any time. Now, aren't you going to introduce me to your friends?'

The sun had just set and all the colour had drained from the hot summer sky when Xanthus the farm manager drove them into the dusty farmyard. Xanthus was a short, leathery freedman with thin fair hair and a permanently worried expression. As the cart rocked to a halt, he jumped down to wedge the wheels. Flavia and the others climbed out of the carriage, stretching and groaning.

The jolting of the cart had produced the usual effect on Flavia: she was bursting to use the latrine. Scuto's intention was the same as hers. He scampered round the farmyard, wagging his tail and sniffing out a suitable spot to relieve himself. He finally decided to take revenge on the big wooden box which had jostled and jolted him for nearly an hour.

Flavia's dog had just lifted his leg against one of the cart's rear wheels when there was a terrifying snarl. Out of the evening shadows streaked an enormous creature.

A huge black wolf was heading straight for Scuto!

SCROLL VII

As the snarling wolf tore through the farmyard, everyone froze. Even Scuto – one leg still lifted – seemed paralysed by fear as the savage creature bore down upon him.

'Ferox! No!' bellowed Flavia's uncle Gaius.

The enormous beast jerked to a halt, as if it had been pulled up short.

Flavia looked closer: it *had* been pulled up short. The monster strained against a leather collar attached to a long iron chain. His eyes bulged with fury and his claws scrabbled at the earth.

Scuto gulped, lowered his leg and backed off. Jonathan and Nubia clutched their own puppies tightly. Nipur was whimpering and Tigris expressed his un-tigerlike terror by wetting his master's tunic.

'Oh Pollux!' swore Jonathan. 'He's widdled down my front.'

As if a spell had been broken, everyone laughed and began to move again. Ferox was the only one not amused. He uttered a series of deep barks which echoed off the farm buildings and stables.

'Come bathe and have some dinner,' shouted Flavia's uncle over the din. 'The slaves will unpack. And don't worry about Ferox. Once he gets to know you, he's no trouble at all.'

Gaius's farm was an ancient but cheerful building with white walls and a red-tiled roof. The living quarters were built round an atrium and a large inner garden. A high wall separated the house from the farmyard and outbuildings.

Next to the kitchen was a simple two-roomed bathhouse. Gaius's house-slaves had heated the water so that the travellers could wash off the dust of the journey and soak their aching limbs. The girls went first, followed by the boys and men.

Clean and refreshed, hair still damp, they found their way to the garden triclinium just as the first few stars pricked the violet sky.

'It is our Sabbath,' Mordecai said to Flavia's uncle. 'Do you mind if Miriam lights the candles?'

'Of course not,' said Gaius, and Mordecai gave him a small bow of thanks.

As the adults reclined and the children took their seats, Miriam remained standing. Pulling a lavender scarf over her curly hair, she recited a Hebrew prayer and lit the candles with a taper.

For a moment everyone was silent. The scent of rose and jasmine drifted in from the inner garden and somewhere a bird sang one sleepy note. The moon hung like a pearl crescent above the cool green leaves of a laurel tree.

Then Gaius's ancient cook Frustilla shuffled in with hot black-bean soup, cold roast chicken and brown bread, while a half-witted house-slave named Rufus began to light the oil-lamps.

As they ate, Gaius asked Flavia if there was anything special she and her friends would like to do while they were in Pompeii.

'We'd like to visit a blacksmith's shop by the Stabian Gate.'

'That's an unusual request for a ten-year-old girl.' Her uncle raised an eyebrow. 'May I ask why?'

'Well, a few days ago we rescued Admiral Pliny –'

'What!' Gaius nearly choked on his soup. 'You rescued Admiral Pliny? The Emperor Vespasian's friend and advisor?'

Flavia nodded. 'He asked us to solve a riddle and find the man who gave it to him.'

'A *riddle*? Before you tell me how you rescued Pliny, can you tell me why on earth the Commander-in-Chief of the imperial fleets wants to solve a riddle?'

Flavia and Jonathan looked at each other and grinned.

'The treasure!'

Jonathan's eyes opened with a start. His heart was pounding and his body was drenched in sweat. At first he thought he was still dreaming. The ceiling of his bedroom was too high and the walls were too close together. The faint scent of fermenting wine drifted through the high window. Somewhere a cock crowed.

Then he remembered. He was at Flavia's uncle's farm. The previous day, the Sabbath, had been a quiet one. They had unpacked and explored the farm. Today they were going into Pompeii to look for the blacksmith called Vulcan.

'Lupus?' he whispered. There was no reply.

Jonathan lifted his head. He was surprised to see Lupus's bed was empty. Tigris was gone, too.

After a moment Jonathan got up and slipped on his tunic and sandals. Groggily he pulled back the curtain in the doorway and walked from the dim atrium into the bright garden. It was a few minutes past dawn and the sky above was lemon yellow. Birdsong filled the air and the cock crowed again.

'Good morning, Jonathan!' said Flavia. 'We were just going to get you.'

'Breakfast is ready.' Miriam smiled at him.

They all sat around a white-painted wrought-iron table under a laurel tree near the well, eating flat brown bread, dates and white cheese. The dogs sat attentively nearby, hoping for scraps. Miriam was pouring out barley water from a jug and Aristo was making notes on a wax tablet.

Jonathan pulled back a chair and sat down heavily.

'Are you all right, Jonathan?' asked Flavia, passing him the plate. 'You look a bit pale.'

'Just a bad dream.' He tore off a piece of bread and tossed it to Tigris. Then he took a handful of dates. 'Are we having lessons today? I thought we were going into Pompeii to find Vulcan.'

'Uncle Gaius says he'll take us later,' said Flavia, 'when he takes my father back to the harbour.'

'Don't worry.' Aristo had seen the look on Jonathan's face. 'It's only a short lesson today.'

The young Greek put down his wax tablet and lifted a large orange and black ceramic pot from the ground. He set it carefully in the centre of the table. On its side was painted a scene from Greek mythology.

Scuto had wandered off with the puppies to explore the garden. Jonathan watched them wistfully.

'This Greek vase is an antique – almost five hundred years old,' Aristo was saying. 'It was used for mixing wine at dinner parties. Flavia's uncle very kindly said I could show it to you this morning. You may look, but – no, Lupus! Don't touch it! It's worth over four hundred thousand sestercii.'

Jonathan sat up straight. 'That's nearly half a million!'

'Precisely,' said Aristo. 'Not only is it old, but it is the work of a master. The artist has decorated this vase in a very clever way, painting the space *behind* the figures black, so that they show up red-orange, the colour of the clay. Then, with a fine brush, he has added the eyes, mouths and other details. This, of course, is the way all the Greek potters decorated their vases five hundred years ago.'

Jonathan and the others brought their faces closer to look at the figures on the big mixing bowl. Suddenly Lupus giggled and pointed.

'Yes,' admitted Aristo ruefully, 'those satyrs are a bit rude. But when you are half-man, half-goat, I suppose you don't need to wear any clothes.'

Flavia giggled, too, and Miriam blushed. Jonathan grinned; he felt better already.

'However,' said Aristo, clearing his throat. 'I haven't brought out this vase to show you naked satyrs. I know you're looking for a blacksmith named Vulcan and I thought you might like to hear the story of his namesake. This figure here – the man riding the donkey – is Vulcan, blacksmith of the gods.'

SCROLL VIII

'Vulcan,' began Aristo, 'was the son of Jupiter and Juno. As the son of the king and queen of the gods, he should have been very fine to look at, but baby Vulcan was small and ugly with a red, bawling face. Juno was so horrified that she hurled the tiny baby from the top of Mount Olympus.'

'What is Muntulumpus?' asked Nubia.

'Mount Olympus,' enunciated Aristo, 'is a mountain in the north of Greece. It's the home of the gods.'

'What happened to the baby?' asked Miriam, her violet eyes wide with concern.

'The baby fell down for a day and a night. Luckily, he landed in the sea. Even so, his legs were damaged as they struck the water and they never developed properly. Baby Vulcan sank like a pebble into the cool, blue depths, where the sea-nymph Thetis found him and took him to her home – an underwater grotto. There she raised him as if he were her own child.'

Aristo paused to take a sip of barley water. 'Vulcan had a happy childhood. Dolphins were his playmates and pearls his toys. Then one day, when he was about your age, he found the remains of a fisherman's fire on the beach. The young god stared in amazement at a single coal, still red-hot and glowing. After a world of cool, watery blues and greens, it was more lovely to him than any pearl.

'Vulcan carefully shut this precious coal in a clam shell, took it back to his underwater grotto and made a fire with it. On the first day, he stared at this fire for hours on end, never leaving it. He fed the flames with seaweed, driftwood, coral and stones. On the second day, he discovered that when he made the fire hotter with bellows, certain stones sweated iron or silver or gold. The third day he beat the cooled metal into shapes: bracelets, chains, swords and shields.

'Vulcan made pearl-handled knives and spoons for his foster-mother. He made a silver chariot for himself and bridles so that seahorses could transport him quickly. He even made slave-girls of gold to wait on him and do his bidding. From that day onwards, he and Thetis lived like royalty.'

Aristo pointed to the vase.

'See, he holds hammer and tongs. That's how you can recognise him. And if you look carefully, you can see that the artist has painted his legs to look too small for his body.'

'He looks sad,' said Miriam.

'But he looks nice, too,' decided Flavia.

'Where's he going?' asked Jonathan.

'He's being escorted back to Mount Olympus. Here's how it happened.

'One day Thetis left her underwater grotto to attend a dinner party on Mount Olympus. She wore a beautiful necklace of silver and sapphires, which Vulcan had made for her. Juno admired this necklace and asked where she could get one.

'Thetis became flustered and Juno grew suspicious. At last the queen of the gods discovered the truth: the baby she had once rejected had now grown up to become the most gifted worker in precious metals the world had ever seen.

'Juno was furious and demanded that Vulcan come home. The smith god flatly refused. However, he did send Juno a most beautiful chair. Made of silver and gold, inlaid with mother-of-pearl, it had a seat like a shell and arms like dolphins.

'Juno was delighted when she received it, but the moment she sat down, her weight triggered hidden springs: metal bands sprung forth to hold her fast. The more she shrieked and struggled, the more firmly the mechanical throne gripped her. The chair was a cleverly designed trap!'

Lupus gave a triumphant bark of laughter and slapped his thigh.

'Serves her right,' agreed Jonathan.

Aristo smiled.

'For three days Juno sat fuming, still trapped in

43

Vulcan's chair. She couldn't sleep, she couldn't stretch, and she couldn't eat.'

'Ewww!' said Jonathan. 'She couldn't use the lavatory either.'

The girls tittered and Lupus guffawed. Aristo gave them a stern look and waited until they were quiet.

'It was Jupiter who finally saved the day. He promised that if Vulcan would return to Mount Olympus and release Juno from the chair, he would give him a wife. And not just any wife, but Venus, the goddess of love and beauty. What man, or god, could resist?'

Aristo pointed to the big vase. 'Here he is riding his donkey back to Olympus, where his mother sits trapped on her throne.'

'Where is Venus?' asked Nubia.

'Probably getting ready for the wedding.'

'Did she love Vulcan?' asked Miriam.

Aristo shrugged. 'Perhaps. But she loved many others too, after all, she is the goddess of love. Later, Vulcan built a smithy under a huge mountain on the island of Sicily. They say that whenever Venus is unfaithful, Vulcan grows angry and beats the red-hot metal with such force that sparks and smoke rise up from the top of the mountain. We call mountains which send forth smoke and fire "volcanoes", after Vulcan.'

'Not really,' snorted Jonathan. 'That's just a story.'

'Is it? If it's not the god Vulcan at his forge which

causes mountains to send up smoke and flames, then what does?'

Flavia raised her hand. 'Pliny says that earthquakes make volcanoes. And earthquakes are caused when the wind is trapped and there is no escape for it.'

'A reasonable explanation,' said Aristo. 'Though I think the myth is more romantic.'

'What about Thetis?' asked Miriam. 'Didn't she miss Vulcan after he went back to Olympus?'

'Vulcan never forgot his foster mother,' answered Aristo. 'He often visited her underwater grotto and that is why he is a god of sea as well as fire. And later – much later – he made her warrior son Achilles the most beautiful armour in the world. But Juno was Vulcan's real mother, and it was right and proper that they be reunited.'

The young Greek leaned back in his chair and smiled at them. 'Lesson finished! I hope it helps in your search for Vulcan.'

It was late morning by the time they set out on their quest for Vulcan.

Flavia and her three friends had settled themselves in the cart along with forty amphoras of wine and a soft layer of sawdust. They had convinced Scuto and the puppies to stay in the cool garden with Miriam. Xanthus drove the cart and the Gemini brothers rode behind.

As they turned off the farm track onto the main

road to Pompeii, they passed a farmer driving his empty cart back from market. He sat beside his young son, and Flavia heard him whisper that Castor and Pollux were in town. The little boy gazed back at the twin riders with his thumb in his mouth and eyes as round as coins.

'Uncle Gaius, why aren't you married?' Flavia leaned back against an amphora and gazed up at her uncle as he rode behind.

Gaius looked down at her in surprise. Then he glanced at his brother.

'Well,' he began, 'When we were younger, we both loved Myrtilla –'

'You loved my mother?' Flavia sat up straight in the cart.

'Yes,' said her uncle Gaius. 'Yes, I did. But she preferred your father.'

SCROLL IX

'It's not quite that simple,' said Flavia's father. 'When pater died, Gaius inherited the farm because he was the eldest. That didn't bother me. I wanted to sail the world.'

'But I prefer plants and animals. I could never dream of making my life on board ship,' said Flavia's uncle. 'I get seasick just watching ships in the harbour.'

'And I'd be a terrible farmer. Your uncle was very generous. He sold some antique vases, and he gave me enough money to buy my ship.'

'I thought if I got Marcus out of the way, I'd have a better chance with Myrtilla,' admitted Gaius with a grin.

'What he didn't realise,' said Flavia's father, 'was that your mother was an adventurer like me. I named my ship after her, and promised to show her the world if she'd marry me.'

Gaius sighed. 'I offered her life on a farm in the most beautiful bay in the world. But . . .' he shrugged.

'And that's why you never married?'

Her uncle nodded and Flavia felt the odd sensation

47

she sometimes got when she really focused on him. He looked so much like her father.

Flavia settled back against her amphora again, and considered that had fate been different, Gaius might have been her father. Her name might have been Julia or Helena. Perhaps she'd be older or younger, with darker hair or different-coloured eyes. But then would she still be Flavia? It made her head hurt just to think about it.

Abruptly, another thought occurred to her: if her mother had married Gaius instead of her father, maybe she wouldn't have died in childbirth. Maybe her mother would still be alive.

There were no festive strollers in the port of Pompeii that morning; it was a busy market day. The *Myrtilla*'s crew and Xanthus loaded the wine aboard the ship, while Flavia's father sacrificed a dove at the harbour shrine of Castor and Pollux. By the time Flavia and her friends had waved the *Myrtilla* out of the harbour, it was almost noon. The sky above was a hard blue, and the heat like a furnace.

Carts were not allowed into Pompeii via the Sea Gate, so Gaius instructed Xanthus to meet them outside the Stabian Gate in an hour.

As they walked from the harbour up the steep incline to the Sea Gate, they had to make way for groups of men in white togas going to the marine baths, just outside the town walls.

'The law courts have probably just finished for the day,' said Gaius, mopping his brow. 'Everything will be closing for lunch soon, so we'll have to hurry. I just want to show you the forum.'

The shade under the arch of the Sea Gate was blessedly cool, and Flavia noticed that the paving stones were wet.

'This town's built on a hill and the fountains constantly overflow,' her uncle explained. 'That's why Pompeii has the cleanest streets in the Roman empire.'

As they emerged from the shadows into the brilliant light of midday, the heat struck Flavia like a blow. Crowds of sweaty men and perfumed women pushed past her on their way home or to the baths.

She tried to keep up with her uncle, but he was used to walking quickly, and already he was disappearing from sight. Flavia grabbed Nubia's hand and looked round for the boys. Lupus was lingering behind, pointing out rude graffiti to Jonathan. At the entrance to the forum, they had to step over a beggar who showed them his diseased leg. Flavia caught a glimpse of red, open sores and her stomach clenched.

Suddenly they were in the forum, a bright open space surrounded by temples and porticoes.

'There's the Temple of Jupiter.' Her uncle gestured towards the north. 'A beautiful sight, isn't it, still decorated for the festival and with Vesuvius rising up behind it . . . Flavia, are you all right? You're as white as a candidate's toga!'

'Yes, Uncle Gaius. I'm just thirsty.'

'Well, come on, then. There are public fountains on the other side of the forum. Follow me.'

Animals were not allowed into the forum and there were barriers to prevent carts from entering. This meant that many people left their horses and donkeys just outside the entrances, causing an almost permanent bottleneck. As the four friends hurried after Gaius, Flavia found herself squashed between a group of bankers in togas and two half-naked slaves carrying the bankers' tables.

'The Stabian baths are to the left there,' Flavia heard her uncle say, but all she could see was a big plank of wood and the folds of togas.

'Absolutely magnificent, but since the big earthquake they still haven't completed all the repairs. Can you imagine? After seventeen years?'

Flavia jumped up and down a few times. When she was up, she could just see Gaius's light brown hair above the other heads in the crowd.

Someone took her right hand. Jonathan. He shouldered one of the bankers aside and moved in front of Flavia, to protect her from jostling.

She could still hear Uncle Gaius up ahead;

'I remember that earthquake well. I was about thirteen, a little older than you. I'll never forget the smell of the sulphur. Like rotten eggs. Up near Misenum a whole flock of sheep was killed by sulphur fumes. Imagine. Five or six hundred sheep, all killed by a smell.'

'I think *I'm* about to be killed by a smell,' muttered Jonathan.

Flavia swallowed and tried to smile. The stench of sweat was overpowering and the blazing sun made it worse. Her heart pounded and her stomach clenched.

Suddenly there was a scuffle somewhere up ahead.

A woman screamed.

The crowd parted to reveal a man wearing a dark turban and robe. He stood in the street looking around with mad eyes. The woman screamed again as the man grasped one of the bankers and shook him by the shoulders.

'God's judgement!' he cried in a hoarse voice. 'It's coming upon us all! The abomination that causes desolation!'

He released the startled banker and clutched at a slave's wrist.

'Doom! Death! Desolation!' he rasped. The slave shook him off with an oath, but the madman persisted. He looked round as the crowd shrank back, then stared straight at Flavia and her friends.

'You!' He pointed towards them. 'You know it, too!'

Please not me, Flavia prayed.

He flung his arms wide in a sweep of black robes ands swooped down on them. His face came nearer and nearer. And stopped inches from Jonathan's.

Flavia saw his red-rimmed eyes stare into Jonathan's and when he opened his mouth to prophesy doom, she smelled garlic and fish on his breath. 'You know it, too!' he said to Jonathan.

Flavia knew she was going to faint.

Suddenly a fist shot out. The madman's chin flew up and back, carrying him with it.

Lupus had knocked him flat.

SCROLL X

Lupus winced and blew on his smarting knuckles.

'Thanks, Lupus,' said Jonathan.

Lupus shrugged and grinned. One of the things he had learned on the streets of Ostia was the effect of a swift blow where chin met neck.

The turbaned man lay in the wet street, staring up at the blue sky and moaning: 'Doom. Death. Desolation.'

'Jupiter's eyebrows!' Flavia's uncle rushed up to them. 'Are you all right? Did that madman hurt you?'

'It's all right, Uncle Gaius. We're fine.' Flavia clutched her uncle's arm and leaned on it gratefully.

'He must be some kind of soothsayer,' said Gaius. He made the sign against evil and guided them around the turbaned man to a nearby fountain.

Lupus plunged his hand into the overflowing fountain basin while the others took turns at the spout. He drank last and as he raised his dripping mouth he heard a woman's voice.

'That man's a Christian. I'm sure of it!'

Lupus wiped his mouth and glanced at Jonathan,

who was watching two soldiers push their way through the crowd.

'The soothsayer's a Christian!' someone else cried out.

'Always prophesying doom!' said the first woman.

The soldiers bent down and the metal strips of their armour flashed as they lifted the turbaned man and dragged him back towards the forum.

'You know the punishment for practising an illegal faith!' called the banker angrily. 'The amphitheatre!'

'Lunch for a hungry lion!' someone else quipped. There was laughter as the crowd began to disperse.

'I think *we* need some lunch,' said Gaius, looking around. 'Ah! That corner snack bar does wonderful chick-pea pancakes. How about it?'

Lupus was hungry, but he wanted to find the blacksmith too, and he knew the shops would be closing soon. He caught Flavia's eye. She nodded to show she understood.

'Uncle Gaius, we're all hungry, but if we don't hurry we might miss Vulcan.'

'All right. Let's find your blacksmith and then we'll eat.'

Even as he finished speaking the gongs began clanging noon; it was time for shops to close and the baths to open.

They followed Gaius as he hurried past several more fountains to the Stabian Way. As soon as they turned onto it, Lupus saw the gate at the bottom.

Keeping to the cool shadows beneath overhanging roofs, he ran ahead, past townhouses on the left and the theatre on his right.

Just before the gate, on the left, were three shops in a row. In the window of the middle shop, above the counter, hung a dazzling selection of pots, pans, lamps and bath scrapers, all bronze, all flashing in the sunlight.

Hearing Lupus's footsteps, a dwarf in a sea-green tunic emerged from the doorway and clanked a string of bronze cowbells.

'Best pans here!' he called out cheerfully. 'Please come in!'

'We're looking for a blacksmith named Vulcan,' cried Flavia, running up.

Lupus grunted at her urgently and pointed to the shop next to it. It did not have a window or a counter, just an open door. But above this doorway someone had painted a scene from Greek mythology: a young man, riding a donkey and carrying his tools. It was the god of blacksmiths: Vulcan.

'Hello?' Flavia peered into the dark smithy. 'Is anyone there?'

'We're closing for the day!' came a gruff voice from inside.

Flavia stepped in, so that she could see better. Nubia and Jonathan stayed behind her, but Lupus squeezed through and slipped into the shop. It was as hot and dark as Hades. The only light came from the doorway behind them and from coals glowing redly on an open hearth.

'We're looking for Vulcan,' she called, feeling foolish even as she said it.

A figure moved out of the darkness – a huge muscular man in a leather apron. He was totally bald and the red coal-light gleamed off his shiny scalp and shoulders.

'Vulcan, is it?' said the gigantic blacksmith in a low growl.

'Yes, please,' replied Flavia politely and took an involuntary step backwards onto Nubia's foot.

'Are you one of them?'

'What?' said Flavia.

'Do you know the way?' The smith bent forward to peer at the three of them. They backed hastily towards the door and into Gaius who stood solidly behind them.

The big smith lifted his head to see Gaius filling the doorway. He straightened himself and for a moment he studied their faces. Then he folded his arms.

'Vulcan doesn't work here any more and don't ask me where he's gone, because I don't know.'

'But we have to find him,' protested Flavia.

'Closing up shop now. You'll have to go. All of you!' The big blacksmith glared at Lupus, who was pointing at some graffiti on the smithy wall. Flavia squinted at it. In the dim red coal-light she could just make out the first two lines: 'My first letter grieves, my second commands . . .'

Suddenly, Flavia knew the answer to the riddle.

Heart pounding, she turned back to the giant, took a deep breath and said:

'*Asine!* You jackass!'

SCROLL XI

'*Asine*,' Flavia repeated loudly. 'Jackass!'

'Flavia!' she heard her uncle's horrified voice behind her. 'Apologise at once!'

But the giant's scowling face had already relaxed into a gap-toothed grin.

'Shhh!' he placed a meaty finger against his lips. 'We can't be too careful, you know.' He glanced around and bent nearer. 'I wasn't lying when I told you Vulcan doesn't work here any more. But he *does* stop in from time to time. You see, he's a travelling smith these days. I could give him a message next time he passes by.'

'A message . . .' said Flavia. 'Yes! We have an important message for him. If you see him, tell him to come to the Geminus Farm on the road to Stabia. We have work for him, don't we, Uncle Gaius? Important work.'

'So the answer to the riddle was *asine*, "jackass",' said Jonathan as they rode home in the cart. 'How did you solve it?'

'Well,' said Flavia, popping the last of a chick-pea

58

pancake into her mouth. 'When we had all the letters but one, I went through the alphabet: *Abine, acine,* and so forth.'

'I did that, too, but I didn't get the answer . . .'

'I thought of *asine,* but it didn't make any sense,' said Flavia, 'until we were in the smithy. Then I remembered the donkey Vulcan rides on, and I knew that must be the word.'

'Of course!' Jonathan hit his forehead with the heel of his hand. 'The missing letter is S which sounds like *es* – "be!", "My second commands . . ." But what does it mean?'

'It's obviously a password or codeword of some sort,' said Flavia. 'It worked with the big blacksmith!'

'I know that!' said Jonathan. 'I mean: how does it help us find a treasure beyond imagining?'

'I don't know,' said Flavia. 'But I'll bet Vulcan the blacksmith does.'

'This was an excellent idea,' said Jonathan later that afternoon. He was testing the weight of a leafy branch.

The four friends were back on the farm, in a fig tree so ancient that it had long ceased to bear fruit. From its upper branches came the liquid notes of Nubia's flute.

Jonathan pushed some large green leaves aside. 'Look!' he said. 'From here we can see anyone coming to the farm, and anyone travelling on the road from Stabia to Pompeii. But they can't see us!'

The old fig tree grew near the edge of an olive grove surrounded by Gaius's vineyards.

'My uncle says we can use those old planks in the tool-shed by the wine press,' added Flavia.

'I've always wanted to build a tree fort,' Jonathan said. 'I'll draw up plans and we can take turns building it and keeping watch.'

Abruptly the flute music stopped and Lupus grunted urgently above them. All Jonathan could see of him were his grubby feet in their too-large sandals.

'What is it, Lupus?' he asked. 'Is Vulcan coming?'

Lupus grunted no. The leaves parted and he pointed to the vines below them.

'You see something in the vineyard?' asked Flavia.

Lupus grunted yes.

'Behold!' said Nubia. 'An orange tunic. But it is now gone.'

'Scuto!' scolded Flavia. 'You're a pathetic watch-dog!'

Scuto, tussling with the puppies in the shade beneath the fig tree, looked up at his mistress and wagged his tail.

'They're all useless,' said Jonathan with a grin.

'It couldn't have been one of my uncle's slaves,' mused Flavia, 'they all wear brown.'

'Then it must have been someone spying on us!' said Jonathan. 'We'll have to keep a sharp lookout from now on.'

★

Over the next few days they spent every free minute working on the tree fort.

At the hottest time of the day, when the adults bathed or napped, the four friends hurried to the leafy coolness of the fig tree to hammer planks, make rope ladders and watch for Vulcan's approach. Once they invited Miriam to help them, but she preferred to stay in the shady house and garden, picking flowers and weaving with Frustilla.

Then, late one morning after their lessons, as they were hurrying off to the tree fort, Gaius's guard dog Ferox finally had his revenge.

After the first evening, Scuto had been careful to give Ferox a wide berth. At first he had behaved in a sensible manner, hugging the farmyard wall fearfully, with his tail firmly between his legs. But as the days passed, his confidence increased.

On the morning in question, Flavia's dog pranced into the farmyard with his tail held high, barked amiably at the hens and began to sniff out an interesting smell. As usual, Ferox shot to the end of his chain and erupted with a torrent of furious barks which Scuto totally ignored. Nose down, Flavia's dog continued to sniff closer and closer to the watchdog, now almost hysterical with rage.

Ferox strained so hard at his collar that his eyes bulged from their sockets and his deep barks were reduced to wheezing gasps. Scuto wandered off nonchalantly, as if the slavering beast at the end of the iron chain were no more threatening than one of the brown hens.

Then Scuto made his mistake. He squatted thoughtfully by the chicken coop, intending to relieve himself of some deep burden. This Ferox could not tolerate. With a last mighty effort, using every fibre of strength in his huge body, he pulled at his iron chain. After a moment there was metallic *ping* as a link of the chain broke.

Like an arrow released from a bow, Ferox sped towards the hapless Scuto.

Flavia had just turned back to call her dog when she saw a golden-brown blur pursued by a huge black streak. They were heading through the vines, towards the coast, and in the time it took Flavia to blink, they had vanished from sight.

SCROLL XII

It was easy enough to follow Ferox's trail: the hound was dragging two yards of iron chain behind him. The four friends and their puppies tracked its snaking path in the dust between the vine rows. Flavia tried not to think of what Ferox might do to Scuto if he caught him.

After half a mile, the trail emerged from the vineyard and ended at the coastal road which marked the border of her uncle's land. There was a distant rider approaching from the direction of Pompeii, but otherwise the road was empty. Across the road and set back from it were the imposing backs of opulent villas overlooking the bay.

The road from Pompeii to Stabia was not wide, but it was well-paved, with tightly fitted hexagonal stones. The daily sea breeze had blown all the surface dust away, and the track left by Ferox's chain ended there.

'Now where?' said Flavia, close to tears. 'Where could he be?'

'Behold!' Nubia pointed. 'Nipur something smells.'

Nipur had been sniffing round the base of a road-side shrine to the god Mercury on the other side of the road. Now he nosed his way through dried grasses and thistles towards the back of one of the seaside villas.

The puppy led them to a high white wall with ancient cypress and cedar trees rising up behind it. In the centre of the garden wall was a solid-looking, wooden door with the words 'DO NOT ENTER' in faded red letters on the wall next to it. Despite the warning, a gap had been scraped in the earth beneath the door.

Flavia uttered a cry. Half of Ferox protruded from this gap. The rear half.

'Your dog is stuck,' came a piping voice from above them. Flavia and her friends looked up in astonishment to see a small girl sitting on the high wall, half hidden in the shade of an umbrella pine.

'I've been waiting for you,' remarked the girl, and added, 'I thought this was the safest place.'

'Have you seen another dog pass this way?' called Flavia desperately. 'One with curly light brown fur?'

The little girl regarded Flavia with eyes as dark and bright as a sparrow's. She was barefoot and dressed in a bright orange tunic.

'Don't worry about Scuto. He's safe inside with my little sisters.'

Flavia whispered a prayer of thanks.

'Wait!' cried Jonathan. 'How did you know Scuto's name?'

'The same way I know you're Jonathan, and you're Flavia and Nubia and Lupus –'

'You're the one who's been spying on us!' cried Flavia.

The little girl smiled brightly. 'Not spying exactly – just watching. My name is Clio.'

At the sound of their voices, Ferox had begun to squirm. He was wedged as tightly beneath the door as a cork in a wine skin. Clio grasped a pine branch and pulled herself up. 'I'll get help,' she offered.

'Wait!' said Jonathan. 'See if you can find some strong rope and – no! get a fishing net!'

Clio grinned, nodded, and scampered off along the top of the high wall as confidently as if it were a broad pavement. Lupus watched her in admiration.

As soon as she was out of sight, the four friends turned their gaze on Ferox, wedged beneath the door. Flavia almost felt sorry for him, but when he began to whimper and scrabble feebly with his hind legs the sight of his quivering black bottom reduced her to helpless laughter.

Impulsively, Lupus picked up a piece of gravel and flicked it at the animal's vulnerable rear.

'Lupus, don't!' giggled Flavia nervously. 'You'll just make him angrier!' Lupus gave her an impish grin. He took another stone and fitted it into the sling Jonathan was teaching him to use.

He had obviously been practising.

The stone hit the watchdog squarely on the bottom. Ferox yelped like a puppy and they all collapsed with mirth.

Suddenly, Ferox began to growl and squirm. This time he tried retreating, inching back towards his tormentors. And this time he succeeded.

Nubia had seen this coming.

As Ferox shook himself off and began to turn, she scooped up Nipur and thrust him at Flavia.

'Hold puppies. Nobody is moving!'

Jonathan nodded and clutched Tigris tightly.

Ferox crouched. A low growl rumbled in his chest.

But before he could leap, Nubia caught his gaze, held it and murmured soothing words in her own language.

After a few moments, she slowly extended her hand – palm down – and took a small but confident step forward. Ferox growled again, but with less conviction. Nubia continued to reassure him. Presently, she took another step forward. The huge dog's hackles gradually flattened and he rose from his crouching position. Nubia took another step.

Ferox sniffed her fingertips, gave a half wag of his tail and allowed his gaze to flicker sideways for a moment. Without taking her eyes from Ferox's face, Nubia crouched and groped in the dust. When her hand closed around the metal links of his chain, she stood again and breathed a small sigh of relief.

It was at that precise moment that Tigris, squirming

in Jonathan's arms, uttered several sharp, defiant barks.

Ferox crouched again, opened his dripping jaws and launched himself at Jonathan.

Flavia screamed and Jonathan instinctively threw himself to one side.

Nubia tried to hold the huge animal back, but was jerked off her feet as the iron chain whipped out of her grasp. Ferox's sharp teeth missed Tigris by a whisker. Snarling with rage, the big dog skidded in the dust and turned to attack again.

As Ferox gathered himself to leap, something like a spear struck him hard on the side. It knocked him to the ground. A heavy oak staff lay in the dust beside the stunned dog.

'Quickly!' called a man's voice. 'The net! Throw the net!'

Flavia looked up in time to see Clio standing on the wall above them. A motion of the girl's arm unfurled a yellow fishing net.

It floated to the ground.

Clio's aim was perfect: as Ferox struggled to his feet, the net enveloped him.

Then Flavia saw a young man lunge forward, grasp the net and give it a deft tug. Ferox's legs flew out from under him. Confused and stunned, the big dog tried to right himself, but the more he thrashed, the more hopelessly entangled he became.

'Get right back, Lupus!' Jonathan scrambled to his feet. 'He might still get loose! Tigris! Come here! You bad dog!' Jonathan gave his puppy a fierce hug.

Flavia helped Nubia up from the ground. 'Are you all right?'

Nubia nodded, but she was trembling.

The garden gate squeaked open and Clio rushed out. She stood with her hands on her hips, looking down at Ferox. 'He's wrapped himself up as tightly as a sausage in a vine leaf,' she observed.

Lupus guffawed and Clio grinned at him.

As Gaius's watchdog thrashed furiously on the ground, Flavia looked up at the strong youth. He wore the one-sleeved tunic of a tradesman and had a chest and arms like Hercules.

'Thank you,' she said solemnly. 'You saved our lives.'

The young man limped cautiously towards Ferox to retrieve his staff. Flavia saw that one of his leather boots was an odd shape. Glancing back towards the road, she saw a donkey tethered to the shrine of Mercury. In its basket-pack were a workman's tools: tongs, a hammer and an axe.

'Vulcan!' she squealed, jumping up and down and pointing at him. 'You're Vulcan the blacksmith!'

SCROLL XIII

Scuto had escaped Ferox only to be captured by Clio's younger sisters. They had pounced on him with cries of delight. After they had bathed, combed and brushed him, they had anointed him with scented oil. Clio rescued him just in time; her sisters had been about to tie pink ribbons to his fur.

Now he hurried furtively through the vineyard, trailing a cloud of jasmine perfume and a small procession.

First came the two puppies, stopping to roll in the dust whenever Scuto did.

Then came Vulcan, riding his grey donkey and pulling Ferox – still cocooned in the yellow fishing net – on a makeshift stretcher of pine branches. Nubia walked beside Ferox, softly playing her flute. Whenever she stopped playing, the big dog began to thrash and moan.

Clio had fallen into step beside Lupus, and was chattering away to him non-stop, waving her arms expansively.

'I wonder how long it will take Clio to realise that Lupus can't speak,' Flavia said to Jonathan with a grin. They took up the rear of the procession.

One of her uncle's field-slaves must have run ahead to alert the farm, for when they emerged from the vines, most of the household was waiting in the farmyard.

Nubia's flute music trailed off and Ferox began to moan again.

'What happened?' said Aristo.

'Are you all right?' asked Mordecai.

'Where's Ferox?' said Gaius.

'Uncle Gaius!' Flavia squealed. 'Ferox broke his chain and we followed him to a villa and he got stuck but then he wiggled out and attacked us but Vulcan saved us!'

'Ferox broke his . . . Who?' said Gaius.

'Vulcan the blacksmith,' said Flavia. 'The one we've been looking for!'

'You're Vulcan the blacksmith?' Gaius asked the youth on the donkey.

But the young man did not reply. He was gazing over their heads, towards the garden. There was a look of awe on his face, as if he had seen something miraculous. Flavia and the others turned to see what he was staring at.

Miriam had just emerged from the garden, her arms full of ivy and fragrant honeysuckle. Dressed in a lavender stola, with her glossy, dark curls pinned up at the neck, Venus herself could not have looked more beautiful.

Although the farmyard was like a furnace in the

noonday heat, Flavia and her friends gathered round Vulcan to watch him mend Ferox's chain. He was crouched over the chain with a pair of pliers. His one-sleeved tunic revealed tanned, oiled shoulders gleaming with sweat. The powerful muscles of his arms and chest bulged as he squeezed the link.

'There. That should hold him.' Vulcan glanced up at Jonathan and Lupus, who were gazing at him with open-mouthed admiration. 'Could one of you bring me a cup of water? I'm very thirsty.'

The boys nodded and both ran off towards the house.

Flavia couldn't take her eyes off the blacksmith. Somehow his neat head seemed all wrong on the powerful body. With his sensitive mouth and long eyelashes, it was as if a sculptor had wrongly put the head of a poet on the body of Hercules. His dark eyebrows met above his nose, giving his face a mournful, brooding look.

And Flavia's gaze kept straying to the strangely shaped boot he wore on his right foot.

Jonathan and Lupus ran empty-handed back out of the garden. 'My sister's drawing cold water from the well,' said Jonathan.

Vulcan nodded and turned to Flavia's uncle, who stood leaning against the shady doorway of the olive press. 'You can put his collar on again, now.'

It had taken Gaius a good half hour to calm his dog and cut off the fishing net.

'I think I'll leave him in his kennel to calm down.' Gaius stepped forward. 'Thank you for saving the children, and for repairing his chain.'

The young blacksmith acknowledged Gaius's thanks with a nod. He wiped the sweat from his forehead with the back of his forearm.

Flavia was desperate to ask Vulcan about the riddle, but there were too many people within earshot, including Clio and some of her uncle's farm slaves.

So she decided to try the codeword.

'*Asine!* You jackass!'

Vulcan turned slowly and looked at her, his eyes smouldering under his single eyebrow. Then he looked back at Miriam, coming towards him with a shy smile and a cup of cold water.

Flavia shivered. It felt as if he had looked right through her.

'Thank you,' Vulcan said quietly to Miriam, and without taking his eyes from her face, he lifted the cup to his lips and drank. Jonathan's sister lowered her gaze.

The shrill cry of the cicadas had ceased some time earlier, and the hot afternoon seemed to be holding its breath. The only sound Flavia could hear was Vulcan swallowing great gulps of cold water.

Suddenly, she felt dizzy and unbalanced, as if she were about to faint. She gasped and reached out for Nubia, who reached for her in the same moment. Clutching at each other, the two girls looked up just in time to see Miriam fall forward into Vulcan's arms!

'What in Hades?' Jonathan lay flat on his back in the dust, and wondered why Vulcan was holding his sister.

It felt as if the farmyard court had been given a brisk shake by a giant's hand. They had all staggered, Jonathan and Clio had fallen down. Doves exploded out of the dovecote and the hens ran clucking out of their coop. In their stables the horses whinnied and in the garden the dogs began to bark.

Vulcan gently set Miriam back on her feet. Her face was as pale as alabaster.

Fine dust from the farmyard had risen in a golden cloud. Now it began to settle again.

'Earth tremor,' explained Flavia's uncle, helping Clio up. He extended his hand to Jonathan and pulled him to his feet. 'Nothing to worry about. We've had quite a few minor quakes this summer. That one wasn't too bad. All the same, Xanthus and I had better have a quick look round the farm to make sure nothing's been damaged. Xanthus!' he called.

Gaius turned away and then turned back.

'I imagine you're all feeling a bit shaken. Miriam, perhaps you could ask Frustilla to prepare lunch now? I'll join you presently. Vulcan and Clio, I hope you'll both join us.'

★

Lupus followed Vulcan through the garden, admiring the smith's muscular back and wondering why he limped. Jonathan's father must have wondered the same thing, for as Vulcan came into the dining-room, Mordecai stepped forward with a look of concern on his face:

'You've hurt yourself. You're limping.'

Vulcan looked flustered. 'It's nothing. I've had it from birth.'

'Please,' insisted the doctor. He gestured for Vulcan to recline and then nodded at Miriam, who had just come in with a copper pitcher and basin. She poured a stream of water onto her father's hands, catching the overflow in the basin. Mordecai dried his hands on the linen napkin over her arm. Then he turned back to Vulcan, who was reclining on one of the low couches.

Lupus and the others tried to see what Mordecai was doing, but he kept his back to them and allowed his loose blue robes to screen Vulcan's foot from their view. Lupus saw the doctor put the blacksmith's boot on the floor and bend his turbaned head over the foot.

'Ah,' murmured Mordecai, almost to himself, 'Clubfoot. Not a terribly bad case . . .' He examined it for a few minutes and then helped Vulcan put the boot back on.

'This could have been corrected shortly after birth, when your bones were still soft.' He dipped his hands in the basin and then turned back, drying them on a napkin. 'It could have been corrected! Did your parents not know that?'

Tears filled Vulcan's eyes, but they did not spill over. His voice was steady as he looked up at Mordecai.

'I don't know who my parents are, sir. I was abandoned at birth.'

SCROLL XIV

Flavia felt miserable. She had called a poor, orphaned, clubfoot a jackass! How could she ever ask him about the treasure now?

Listlessly, she pushed some black olives around the rim of her dish. It was terribly hot and suddenly she had no appetite.

Her uncle Gaius strode in from his inspection of the farm and quickly rinsed his hands in the copper basin. He threw himself on the couch next to Aristo and helped himself to a slice of cheese.

'Not too much damage to the farm,' he remarked through his first mouthful. 'A few shattered roof tiles and a crack in the olive press. I'm glad you got our message, Vulcan. I really could do with the services of a blacksmith for a few days. I hope you don't mind staying in the slave quarters?'

'Not at all,' said the smith, with a quick glance at Miriam.

There was another pause.

Nubia broke the silence. 'Are you the god Vulcan from Muntulumpus?'

Vulcan almost smiled.

'No. Vulcan is just my nickname. It's not hard to guess how I got it. I don't like it, but it's something I have to live with.'

Flavia swallowed. If he didn't like being called Vulcan, he probably didn't like being called a jackass.

The smith took a small piece of cheese and then put it down again. 'I don't know my real name,' he said. 'They say a slave-girl found me wrapped in swaddling clothes beside the banks of the river Sarnus. She gave me to her master and he gave me to one of his freedmen, a blacksmith. My adoptive parents didn't mind my foot. They loved me as if I had been their own son and they gave me the name Lucius. But no one has called me that since my parents died.'

'I'm adopted, too,' said Clio. She was sitting at the table between Lupus and Flavia. 'We're all adopted. All nine of us.'

'Extraordinary,' murmured Mordecai, and then to Vulcan. 'Please continue.'

'There's not much more to tell. We moved to Rome when I was still a baby. I grew up there. My father taught me to be a blacksmith and my mother taught me how to read and write. They died a year ago, when I was sixteen. After I settled their affairs, I moved back here to search for my real parents.'

'My real parents are dead,' said Clio, taking a handful of olives. 'Father says they died in a plague. I never even knew them.'

'Do you want revenge on your parents for abandoning you?' Jonathan asked Vulcan.

'Jonathan!' chided Mordecai.

Vulcan lowered his head and then looked at Jonathan from under his long eyelashes.

'No. I don't want revenge. I have forgiven my true parents. But I want to find them. That's why I came back to Pompeii. For the past year I have looked everywhere in the town, but haven't found them yet. So when Brutus the travelling blacksmith died last month, I bought his donkey. Now I can visit all the farms and villages in the area. If my parents are still here, I know I will find them!' The muscles of his arm bulged as he clenched his fist.

'But how will you recognise them?' asked Jonathan.

'I believe . . .' said Vulcan, and stopped. 'I don't know,' he said finally, 'but I must find them. I must!'

'Why haven't you asked Vulcan about the treasure yet?' Jonathan asked Flavia after lunch.

They had taken Clio to the tree fort, while the adults were having their midday siesta. Jonathan sat cross-legged on the newly-built wooden platform. He was sharpening the point of an arrow with a small knife.

'Treasure?' came Clio's voice from the leaves above. 'What treasure?'

Flavia rolled her eyes at Jonathan. 'That's one

reason I haven't mentioned it! Also, I think he's angry with me for calling him a jackass.'

'That was pretty . . . bold of you,' admitted Jonathan.

'Treasure?' said Clio again, and jumped onto the platform beside Flavia.

So Flavia told Clio all about the riddle and the treasure.

'That's why you called him a jackass,' said Clio, and tipped her head to one side. 'Who did you say gave you the riddle?'

'Our friend Pliny. He's a famous admiral who's written dozens of books.'

'He told us about the riddle because we saved his life,' added Jonathan.

Clio's eyes sparkled. 'Is he a fat old man with white hair and a funny voice?'

Lupus barked with laughter from his treetop perch, and Nubia giggled behind her hand.

'He's not fat!' cried Flavia, sitting up a little straighter. 'He's just a bit . . . stout.'

'Do you know him?' Jonathan asked Clio.

'Of course' she chirped. 'He knows my parents and often stays at our villa. In fact, he's coming to dinner in a few days.'

'He is?' cried Flavia. 'I wish we could come, too. Then we could tell him we've found his blacksmith and almost solved the riddle!'

Clio looked at Flavia with her bright black eyes and

tipped her chin up decisively. 'Then I'll send you all an invitation.'

'In that case,' said Flavia, 'we'd better find out about the treasure!'

'You'll find the blacksmith in the toolshed by the wine cellar,' said Xanthus the farm manager.

Flavia knew the toolshed. It was a dark, cool room full of pruning hooks, plough shares, hoes, picks and various pieces of tackle for cart and horse. When they opened the battered wooden door and peeped in, Vulcan was nowhere in sight. But someone had been there recently. The puppies pushed through Flavia's legs and sniffed round a newly cleared space and a half-built brick furnace against one wall.

'Shhh!' said Jonathan suddenly. 'Do you hear that?'

They all listened. From the cellars on the other side of the toolshed came a bubbling groan, interspersed with curses and mutters.

'It's horrible,' said Clio. 'What is it?'

A shudder shook Nubia and she gripped Flavia's arm.

Even Scuto whimpered.

Jonathan swallowed and looked at them. 'It sounds like someone is being murdered!'

SCROLL XV

Flavia laughed. 'Don't worry,' she said. 'It's just the grape juice in the barrels. It makes that noise as it turns into wine. Sometimes the barrels practically shout. Come on!'

She led them across the beaten earth floor of the toolshed and pushed open the door to the cellars. It was a vast room with thick walls: cool, dark and musty. As they stepped inside, the damp scent of fermenting wine filled Flavia's nostrils and made her slightly dizzy.

Vulcan was there in the gloom, leaning on his staff and speaking quietly to three farm-slaves. When he saw Flavia he stopped talking to them.

'We were just getting more bricks,' he said to Flavia, and nodded towards a pile of bricks. The three slaves hurriedly began taking bricks for the furnace back into the toolshed. Vulcan limped to the doorway to supervise them.

'Did you want me?' he said to Flavia. Although his voice was soft, his dark eyebrows made him look quite stern.

The farm-slaves were passing bricks through the

doorway. Behind them the wine in the barrels snarled and groaned. Despite herself, Flavia shivered, too.

'No, it doesn't matter,' she said, backing out of the room. 'It can wait.'

'What's the matter?' said Jonathan, a minute later. 'Why didn't you ask him about the treasure?'

'Um . . . the slaves,' said Flavia. 'I couldn't ask him in front of them. We'll have to get him alone.'

But as the day progressed the young blacksmith always had at least one slave nearby and Flavia had to resign herself to waiting.

That night Flavia dreamt of her dead mother Myrtilla.

In her dream, they were back in her garden in Ostia, on a summer's evening. Her mother and father sat beneath the fig tree by the fountain, laughing, talking and watching Flavia play with the twins, now Lupus's age.

Flavia had woken at the darkest hour, full of despair, knowing that her mother and dead brothers were only shadows, wandering the cold grey Underworld and chirping like bats. She had tried to replace that terrible image with her dream of them all in a secret, safe and sunny garden. But it was no good. Hot tears squeezed out from the corners of Flavia's eyes, wetting her cheeks and running down into her ears. As she stared into the darkness she knew that she would give all the treasure in the world, everything she had, even her life, if only she could make that dream come true.

The morning of the Vinalia – the late summer wine festival – dawned a glorious pink and blue, but Flavia awoke feeling drained after her restless night. Nubia and the dogs were already up, presumably gone to breakfast. Listlessly, Flavia splashed lukewarm water on her face from the jug in the corner and padded out to the garden for lessons.

The others were crowding round the wrought-iron table examining something. Even the dogs seemed interested. As Flavia approached, Nubia lifted her neat, dark head and called out:

'Flavia! Come see what appears outside Miriam!'

Flavia sighed and quickened her step. The others moved aside to let her see.

On the table was a small wooden cage with a tiny door on one side and a handle on top. Inside perched a bright-eyed little sparrow.

'Oh!' cried Flavia. 'He's lovely! Where did he come from?'

'He just appeared outside Miriam's bedroom door this morning!' said Jonathan, and added, 'Aristo says it means Miriam has an admirer!'

'Who is it, Miriam?' asked Flavia; already her dream was fading. 'Who is your admirer?'

Miriam flushed. 'I don't know.'

Aristo smiled at Miriam. 'A sparrow is the traditional gift of a man to his sweetheart,' he said. 'The poet Catullus even wrote a poem about a sparrow that he gave to his beloved. He talks about the little bird on his girlfriend's lap, hopping about now here and now there.'

'Oh, do you think it's tame?' breathed Flavia.

'Probably,' said Aristo. 'Shall we see?'

He eased open the delicate cage door and held his forefinger just outside. The sparrow cocked his head and regarded the large finger with a bright eye. He hopped to the door and cheeped. Then he hopped onto Aristo's finger. Flavia started to squeal with excitement, but Nubia put a restraining hand on her arm.

Very slowly, Miriam put her elegant white finger next to Aristo's, so that they barely touched. After a moment, the sparrow hopped on to Miriam's finger. Scuto, his eyes fixed on this feathered morsel, gave a wistful whine.

'Oh!' giggled Miriam. 'He tickles.'

'Sit down,' whispered Jonathan. 'See if he hops on your lap now here and now there!'

'Not with the dogs licking their chops like that.' Flavia laughed.

'I take dogs away,' said Nubia solemnly.

'I'll come with you.' Flavia felt much more cheerful. Now she had two mysteries to uncover:

Vulcan's treasure, and the identity of Miriam's secret admirer.

*

There were many things Nubia did not understand about the new land she lived in.

When Flavia's uncle took them all into Pompeii later that morning to celebrate the Vinalia, Nubia did not understand why the priest on the temple steps crushed a handful of grapes over the bleeding carcass of a lamb. When they went to the theatre, she did not understand why the men on the stage wore masks while the women in the audience left their faces uncovered.

Afterwards, when they returned to the farm, she did not understand why on this particular day they ate roast lamb outside, sitting on old carpets near the vines beneath the shadows of the olive grove. She did not understand how Flavia could hand her uncle a piece of bread with the left hand. In her country this was a grave insult, for the left hand was used to wipe the bottom. And she did not think she would ever understand how the Romans could allow a wise old woman like Frustilla to wait on strong young men like Aristo and Vulcan.

But one thing Nubia did understand was the look between a girl and her lover. She had seen the same look many times at the spice market, when all the clans met together to trade.

By the end of the day, as they all walked back through the cool vine rows beneath the pale green sky of dusk, Nubia knew not only that Miriam was in love, but with whom.

SCROLL XVI

Clio had promised them an invitation to the dinner party and sure enough, just as they finished their music lesson the next morning, they heard a banging on the rarely-used front door. Presently a spotty teen-aged slave in a white tunic wandered into the garden. For a few moments he stared at Miriam open-mouthed. Then he remembered himself.

Gaius and Mordecai appeared in the library door-way as the young slave recited his message in a loud voice:

'Titus Tascius Pomponianus invites his neighbour Gaius Flavius Geminus Senior to dinner at the Villa Pomponiana.

'Please bring your family and house guests to my home at the tenth hour tomorrow for a light dinner. The starter will be mussels in sweet wine sauce and the main course a fine turbot caught only yesterday. There'll be quails' eggs, camel's cheese and imported Greek olives.

'My children will play music for your entertainment and our guest of honour will be the Admiral Pliny, on active command of the fleet at Misenum.'

The slave glanced at Miriam, licked his lips nervously and continued,

'My young mistress Clio Pomponiana adds that the young ladies of Gaius's household are invited to bathe . . .' here the young slave's voice broke and he continued an octave higher, '. . . to bathe with her at the ninth hour in the private baths of the villa.'

'I think he means us,' Flavia giggled to Nubia and Miriam.

'Can we go, father?' Miriam said. 'Tomorrow's the Sabbath.'

'Is the villa near enough to walk to?' asked Mordecai.

'Easily,' said Gaius.

Mordecai smiled. 'Very well. I should like to meet Admiral Pliny again.'

'Tell your master we accept his kind invitation with pleasure,' said Gaius with a solemn bow.

After the blushing slave left, Flavia's uncle clapped his hands and rubbed them together energetically. 'Tascius has been in that villa for over a year and this is the first invitation I've had. I owe it all to you and your friends, Flavia!'

Flavia still hadn't been able to get Vulcan on his own, but the next morning there was another clue about Miriam's secret admirer.

Jonathan's sister had just set the breakfast platter on

the table. She was wearing a grey-blue stola with a lilac shawl tied round her slender waist, humming to herself. Flavia sighed: she would never be that elegant and graceful.

Suddenly Jonathan caught his sister's wrist and held it for a moment. Miriam was wearing a silver bracelet set with amethysts.

'It's beautiful,' said Flavia. 'Is it new?'

Miriam blushed and then nodded.

'Who gave it to you?' asked Jonathan sharply.

Miriam shrugged.

'It appears outside your bedroom?' Nubia asked.

Miriam nodded.

'Why are you getting all these presents?' scowled Jonathan. Flavia knew his nightmares had put him in a bad mood.

In the fig tree above them a bird trilled sweetly as Aristo rushed into the garden. He looked sleepy and rumpled, but handsome in a fawn coloured tunic with matching lace-up boots.

If Miriam was silver, thought Flavia, Aristo was bronze.

'Sorry,' he said, pulling back his chair. 'I had a broken night, and I'm afraid I overslept.' He glanced at Miriam.

'Lovely bracelet,' he said. 'Is it new?'

Later that day, a few hours after noon, Nubia ran into the garden from the farmyard. As the gate banged shut, Flavia looked up from Pliny's scroll of famous mysteries. The boys had taken the dogs hunting and all the adults were still resting after lunch.

'Vulcan is in the stables,' said Nubia breathlessly. 'Being all alone.'

'At last!' said Flavia. She left the scroll on the table and ran after Nubia.

Vulcan nodded at the girls as they pushed open the stable door. He had taken his donkey from one of the stalls and was grooming it.

Nubia went straight to the creature to watch Vulcan brush it, but Flavia hoisted herself up on one of the stalls, and drummed her feet on the wooden half-door. She hoped he'd forgiven her for calling him a jackass in front of Miriam.

'Vulcan . . .' She casually nibbled a piece of straw, 'have you ever met Admiral Pliny?'

'I don't think so.' Vulcan was brushing the donkey's back with long firm strokes.

'He knows you.'

Thin shafts of golden sunlight pierced the dusty air and made coins of light on the stable floor. There was a pungent smell of sweet hay and sour mash, of horse dung and saddle oil.

'I might have met him,' said the smith carefully. 'Many of the rich and famous have summer houses in Pompeii.'

Flavia took a deep breath. 'Do you remember giving any of them a riddle?'

Vulcan stopped brushing and looked up at her. 'So that's why you called me a jackass . . .'

'Pliny said you told him that solving the "jackass riddle" would lead to "a treasure beyond imagining" . . .'

Vulcan handed Nubia the curry comb and indicated that she should take over. Nubia happily brushed the donkey's velvet-grey coat.

'I call him Modestus,' Vulcan said, stroking the donkey's long nose, 'because he is a humble creature. He will carry any burden you care to put on him. At the baker's, he will patiently circle a millstone for his whole life, never complaining, just walking. And in the spring, when the donkey gets a new coat, there is a cross on his back. See? Just there where Nubia is brushing. The cross, too, is a symbol of sacrifice and submission.'

Nubia stopped brushing for a moment. 'What is submission?' she asked.

'It's when you allow people to do things to you even though you are strong enough to resist. Like some slaves.'

Vulcan turned to Flavia.

'The donkey is also a symbol of peace. If a king rides on a horse, that means he comes to make war. But if he rides on a donkey, he comes in peace.'

Flavia frowned and jumped down off her perch.

'But how does the donkey lead to treasure?'

Vulcan turned his dark eyes on her. 'You seem to be

a rich girl, Flavia Gemina. You are of good birth. You have your own slave. Why do you need riches?'

The question stumped Flavia.

'Tell me, Flavia Gemina,' continued Vulcan, folding his muscular arms. 'What would be your greatest treasure?'

'A roomful of giant rubies and emeralds and pearls. And gold coins . . .'

'That's what most people say. But think again. What, for you, would be the best treasure, a real treasure, a treasure beyond imagining?'

Behind Flavia the stable door squeaked open and Vulcan looked over her shoulder. His expression changed.

Flavia turned to see Miriam standing in the stable doorway. She was wearing her prettiest violet stola with an apricot shawl. 'Hello, Vulcan,' she said softly, and then to the girls, 'I've been looking for you everywhere. It's almost the ninth hour and time for us to go to Clio's. If we don't hurry, we'll be late!'

Flavia, Nubia and Miriam hurried through the hot vineyards and across the coastal road to find Clio waiting by the back gate of the Villa Pomponiana. An older girl stood beside her.

'Oh good! You're here,' cried Clio. 'I was beginning to worry . . . This is Thalia, my eldest sister. She's fourteen. That's about your age isn't it, Miriam?'

Miriam nodded.

'Thalia's engaged to be married!' said Clio. 'Show them your ring.'

With her protruding eyes and wide mouth, Thalia reminded Flavia of a cheerful frog. She proudly held out her left hand and they all admired her engagement ring: two clasped hands engraved in a garnet. Then Thalia took Miriam's arm and led the way through the shady garden to the bath complex.

Entering the baths of the Villa Pomponiana was like stepping underwater. Painted fish swam across blue walls. On the floor, black and white mosaic tritons pursued laughing sea nymphs. The girls stripped off, and two female bath-slaves took their clothes to be hung, brushed and scented.

Shyly at first, the naked girls made a circuit of the four rooms.

In the first room, they soaked in a green marble pool full of warm, vanilla-scented water. Then they moved into the steam room, where they sat for as long as they could bear on hot cedarwood benches. After the cold plunge they hurried into the last room, where the two slave-girls were waiting with soft linen bath-sheets.

The solarium, with its thick glass skylight, marble slabs and resting couches, was where bathers were scraped, massaged, manicured and coiffed. It led back into the warm room, and the circuit could be done all over again.

Once relatively dry, the girls rubbed scented oil over their bodies.

'Your heels are a bit rough,' commented Thalia, eyeing Flavia's feet. 'Would you like Gerta to pumice them?'

'What's pumice?'

'It's a special stone imported from Sicily,' said Thalia, beckoning one of the slaves with her finger.

'Oh!' cried Flavia, taking the small grey brick. 'It's so light! But it's hard. It looks like an old sponge!' She let Nubia hold it and then gave it back to Gerta.

'It tickles!' Flavia laughed as the slave-girl briskly rubbed the pumice-stone against her heel, but afterwards her heels felt silky smooth. She lay back on one of the couches, wrapped in a soft linen bath-sheet, and as she waited her turn for a massage she pondered Vulcan's question.

Presently the bath-slaves proved their skill as hair-dressers. Quickly and confidently, one pinned up Miriam's cloud of black curls in a simple but beautiful style and the other arranged Thalia's rather frizzy brown hair to look almost as elegant as Miriam's. Nubia watched them with interest.

When their hair was done, Thalia looked at Miriam and sighed. 'You're disgustingly beautiful,' she said cheerfully. 'I'll bet you could win any man you wanted to.'

'Miriam already has dozens of admirers!' said Flavia. She tried to look at Thalia without moving her head because Gerta had begun to arrange her hair. 'Someone gave Miriam a sparrow and a bracelet and all my uncle's farm-slaves stare whenever she goes by.'

'Are you in love, Miriam?'

Miriam blushed.

'Don't try to hide it,' said Thalia. 'I can always tell.'

Miriam gave a tiny nod.

Flavia jerked her head round and she got an ivory hairpin in her scalp.

'Ow! You're in love? Who is he, Miriam?'

But at that moment the table began to shake and tremble. Flavia stared as a bronze hand-mirror shimmied across its surface, slid over the edge and clattered onto the mosaic floor. Her chair was shaking, too. She was just about to ask the slave-girl to stop when Thalia screamed,

'Earthquake! Run! Run for your lives!'

SCROLL XVII

Clean and perfumed, but naked apart from the bath-sheets clutched round them, the girls stood in the hot courtyard while the villa shuddered around them.

'Father! Help!' screamed Thalia. 'FATHER!'

Within moments, a man with fierce eyebrows and short grizzled hair rushed into the courtyard. The quake had obviously interrupted his preparations, too. He was wearing a tunic, but he was barefoot and his toga was slung over his shoulder like a blanket.

'Don't panic, girls!' he commanded. 'Remain in the open. Nothing to be frightened of. Just a tremor. Look! It's over already.'

Thalia had thrown herself sobbing into her father's arms.

'There, there. Told you not to worry about these tremors. Look! Clio's not afraid . . .' He held Thalia at arm's length and examined her red and swollen face. 'Better now, my beauty?'

Thalia sniffed and nodded, and her father turned to Flavia and Miriam.

'Hello, girls!' His broad smile revealed a finely crafted set of wooden false teeth. 'Titus Tascius

Pomponianus, master of this household. Sorry your bath was interrupted by tremors. They're common in this part of the world. Now. I suggest you put some clothes on. The other guests have arrived. Nearly time for dinner!'

The vast, airy dining room of the Villa Pomponiana was open on three sides. Its roof was supported by tall white columns with painted black bases. Gauzy linen curtains could be drawn to dim the room if the light was too bright, but now the setting sun was screened by seaside pines, so the curtains were open.

Flavia's jaw dropped as she gazed out between the columns.

The view was stunning. A sloping lawn glowed yellow-green in the late afternoon sunlight and drew her gaze down to the indigo blue bay with Mount Vesuvius beyond.

As she turned away from the view, Flavia saw that everyone else was already there. Lupus and Jonathan, dressed in their best white tunics, were seated at a large marble table with seven dark-haired girls. Mordecai, Aristo and her uncle were reclining. And there was another familiar face.

'Admiral Pliny!'

The admiral was just as Flavia remembered him: plump and cheerful, with a white fringe of hair and intelligent black eyes. His faded purple tunic was the same one he'd worn at his Laurentum villa, and the same Greek scribe stood behind him with a portable ink pot.

'Flavia Gemina!' wheezed Pliny. 'How delightful to see you again.'

Flavia flushed with pleasure, delighted that the admiral had remembered her name.

'Admiral Pliny, we've solved your riddle and found – hey!' A steward was guiding her firmly towards the table and Pliny had turned away to speak with Tascius.

'Flavia, Miriam and Nubia, I'd like you to meet my sisters,' said Clio, 'Melpomene, Calliope, Euterpe, Terpsichore, Erato, Polyhymnia, and – Urania leave Lupus alone! Besides, that's my seat, so move over!'

'Your sisters are named after the nine muses?' asked Flavia as she took her seat.

Clio nodded and turned to Lupus. '*I'm* named after the muse of history.'

Three female kitchen-slaves padded back and forth across the room, bringing in appetisers and wine. The prettiest one handed out fragrant garlands of dark ivy and miniature white roses. There were garlands on nineteen heads, and a twentieth garland lay between Pliny and Tascius on the central couch. It should have adorned the head of Tascius's wife, but she was late returning from an outing.

Frog-faced Thalia was the only daughter old enough

to recline. She had found a place on the couch beside Aristo. Flavia noticed that although she was engaged, she kept fluttering her eyelashes at him.

Behind each of the three couches stood a slave, ready to cut meat from the bone, retrieve a fallen napkin, refill the empty wine-cups or, in the admiral's case, take notes.

'You must forgive me,' Pliny announced to the company in his light voice, 'if I dictate the occasional line to my scribe. I am completing a study of Roman religion and have vowed to finish it before the Saturnalia four months hence.'

Tascius showed his wooden teeth in a rather stiff smile. 'We know you hate being separated from your stylus and tablets, admiral.' He turned to the others. 'The admiral's written seven complete works. At least a hundred scrolls altogether. His first book was a biography of my father. That's how we met.'

Pliny waggled his forefinger. 'Not quite accurate, my dear Titus. My first book was a manual on how to throw javelin from horseback.'

'I know the one,' said Flavia's uncle from his couch. 'It was required reading when I did my military service.'

Pliny looked pleased. 'I dare say the book I'm writing now will be my greatest yet. My *Natural History* was only thirty-seven volumes. This is now approaching fifty.'

He paused as the slave-girls served the starters:

honey-glazed quails' eggs in fish sauce, squares of camels'-milk cheese and purple olives from Kalamata.

As the others ate, Clio stood up to sing. She was accompanied by Erato on the lyre, and her younger sister Melpomene on the double flute. Clean and with her hair pinned up, Clio looked like a different person. Her voice was high and sweet, and as she confidently sang a popular song called 'The Raven and the Dove', the diners nodded their approval at one another.

Tascius gazed at his adopted daughters affectionately and when Clio finished singing he clapped almost as enthusiastically as Lupus.

'Tell us how you come to have such a large family,' Flavia's uncle Gaius said to Tascius, when the applause had died down. 'And such a talented one!'

The former soldier rubbed the palm of his hand over his short cropped hair.

'My wife,' he said. 'All due to her soft heart. We had a baby, but he was stolen in infancy. Slave-traders, we presume. Never received a ransom note.'

'Your baby was stolen?' cried Flavia, sitting up straight. 'How did it happen?' She noticed her uncle Gaius shaking his head at her and frowning. But Tascius didn't seem offended.

'We were at our Herculaneum villa,' he said. 'Rectina – my wife – was sleeping in her bedroom with the baby. We think there were two of them. One must have passed the baby through the window to his accomplice. When Rectina woke from her nap, the baby was gone. We punished the household slaves, posted a reward, but he was never found.'

'It was a boy?' Flavia asked, ignoring her uncle's warning scowl.

'Yes' said Tascius. 'Just a few weeks old. Rectina was devastated.'

'I apologise for my niece's curiosity,' said Gaius. 'As your guests it's not –'

'No, no. Not offended. Reason my wife and I adopted all these beautiful children. At first we thought we could have others. But they never came. A few years after we lost our son, Rectina brought home a baby girl. An orphan. I called her Thalia.' He smiled at his eldest daughter.

'After that, people kept bringing us abandoned children. I'm a keen musician. Named my girls after the Muses and taught them how to play.'

'Don't you have any sons?' asked Jonathan.

'Baby boys aren't often abandoned,' said Tascius. 'Besides, we always hoped to find our own son.'

He was interrupted by murmurs of approval as the three serving-girls struggled into the dining-room with the main course: an enormous turbot on a silver platter.

'Excuse me,' Pliny said, licking creamy dill sauce from his thumb. 'This delicious turbot has just reminded me of something.'

He snapped his fingers and said over his shoulder. 'Phrixus. New heading: the Vulcanalia. Vulcan, the god of fire and the forge, is important in the months of late summer, when the ground is driest and a careless spark can set a granary on fire and destroy its contents in minutes. During his festival – the Vulcanalia – living fish are thrown on a fire as a substitute for the life of each person. The festival is particularly prominent in the town of Ostia, whose many granaries are the basis of its wealth.'

'We celebrate the Vulcanalia, too,' said Tascius. 'It's the day after tomorrow. Why don't you join us, admiral? Why don't you all come along?'

He looked around at them. 'We hold the fish sacrifice down on the beach. I'm the priest of Vulcan for this region. Because the god requires only the lives of the fish and not their flesh, we provide plenty of wine and make quite a feast of it. Everyone comes, rich and poor.'

'Why, yes!' The admiral clapped his hands in delight. 'I'd love to come.'

'And we will bring Vulcan,' announced Flavia.

They all stared at her.

'Do you mean a statue of the god?' Tascius frowned.

'I do believe she means the blacksmith they call Vulcan,' said Admiral Pliny in his breathy voice, dabbing his mouth with a napkin. 'Have you located him?'

Flavia nodded. 'We solved the riddle you gave us and we found the blacksmith named Vulcan.'

'Remarkable!' said the admiral. 'And the treasure?'

'Well,' said Flavia. 'We're not exactly sure what the treasure is yet . . . But Vulcan's at our farm right now.'

'I look forward to seeing him again,' said the admiral. 'Now, Flavia Gemina, tell us how you and your friends solved the riddle.'

SCROLL XVIII

The sun had long set and the white columns surrounding the dining-room glowed gold in the light of a dozen oil-lamps. Through the columns and beyond the pine torches which illuminated the lawn, the bay gleamed like wet black marble, reflecting a thousand spangles of light. It was difficult to see where the lights of luxury villas stopped and the stars began.

Tascius had just ordered torch-bearing slaves to escort Gaius's party home and everyone was rising from couch and chair, when a tall woman in a peacock blue stola and black shawl swept into the room.

'So sorry I'm late, everyone,' she said in a gracious, well-modulated voice. 'I've been settling affairs at my villa.' She was a dark, attractive woman in her early forties, with a straight nose, long eyelashes and dark hair piled high in a complicated arrangement of curls.

'My dear Pliny.' She kissed the admiral's cheek, then turned to smile at Gaius and Mordecai.

'Rectina,' said Tascius. 'Don't believe you've met our neighbours. Gaius Flavius Geminus. Owns the estate which backs onto our villa. His niece Flavia. His guest Doctor Mordecai ben Ezra . . .'

Flavia stared at Rectina. There was something terribly familiar about her. She was certain she had seen her before. But where?

In the middle of the night, Jonathan woke Flavia. He nudged her shoulder, careful not to spill any of the hot oil from his clay lamp.

'What? What is it, Jonathan?' she mumbled. 'Have you had another nightmare?'

Jonathan shook his head and put his finger to his lips. 'Lupus has something to show you.'

At the foot of Flavia's low bed, Scuto blinked and yawned. Then he rested his head on his paws and sighed. Nubia yawned, too. She pushed back her covers, rose stretching and sat beside Flavia.

'Go on Lupus, show them,' whispered Jonathan. Lupus emerged from the shadows by the door and squatted beside Flavia's bed. He flipped open his wax tablet and began to draw.

'You've drawn Vulcan!' Flavia yawned. 'It's good!'

'He's not finished,' said Jonathan. 'Watch.'

Lupus glanced round at them, eyes glittering sea-green in the flickering lamplight. With a few strokes of the stylus he made Vulcan's mouth fuller and more feminine and thinned out the eyebrows. Finally he added elaborately curled hair and a head scarf.

'Great Neptune's beard!' said Flavia. 'With that mouth and hair, Vulcan looks just like Clio's mother . . . her adoptive mother, I mean.'

105

'Rectina,' said Jonathan.

'But that can only mean –'

Jonathan nodded. 'Rectina must be Vulcan's mother and –'

'Tascius must be his father!' cried Flavia. 'We've found Vulcan's long-lost parents!'

Long after Nubia's breathing had become slow and regular again, Flavia lay awake thinking about the plan she had devised.

She was far too excited to sleep.

Besides, she needed to use the latrine.

She got up and padded soundlessly through the atrium and into the kitchen. Ashes still glowed deep red on the hearth but they didn't provide much light. Flavia felt her way through to the latrine, with its polished wooden seat and hole.

She was just coming back out of the kitchen when she heard a noise – the sound of footsteps and the garden gate.

It must be Miriam's secret admirer leaving another token of his love!

The sky above the garden was charcoal grey, with one or two stars still burning faintly in the west. The chill breeze that often heralded sunrise touched her face and bare arms. Flavia crept silently along the columned walkway, the luminous white chips in the mosaic floor guiding her way.

When she reached the gate, she carefully undid the

latch and opened it. Peering through the predawn gloom across the farmyard, she was just in time to see a figure disappear into the stables. Quietly Flavia eased open the gate and stepped out.

Suddenly she remembered Ferox and froze. But he was nowhere in sight. Someone must have locked him in his kennel.

Flavia crept across the farmyard, the powdery dust cool between her toes. As she drew closer, she heard voices. A light flared and then burned dimly from the small stable window.

Peering through the window, she could just make out a figure standing beside the donkey's stall.

It was Mordecai.

An oil-lamp hung from a hook on the rafters above him and lit an open scroll in his hands. His eyes were closed and he was rocking forwards and backwards with little movements, chanting. A few other oil-lamps created globes of light in the dim space and Flavia caught a whiff of frankincense.

The others, facing Mordecai with their backs to Flavia, were harder to make out. Flavia could distinguish Miriam by the pale scarf draped over her head. And Jonathan stood next to her. The bent figure was probably the old cook Frustilla, and Flavia thought she saw Xanthus, too.

Mordecai stopped rocking and chanting. He briefly bowed his head and kissed the scroll. Then he stood to one side as another figure limped towards him.

It was Vulcan.

The smith stood at the front and began to sing in a light, clear voice. The others joined him, lifting their hands in the air. They were worshipping something.

Flavia knew that Jonathan and his family were Christians. She remembered Jonathan telling her about a shepherd god, but she saw no image. She squinted to find the altar or statue they were praying to. But the only thing they were facing – apart from Vulcan and Mordecai – was the donkey Modestus, dozing peacefully in his stall.

Suddenly she understood.

One of their gods must be a donkey.

They were worshipping a jackass!

SCROLL XIX

Flavia intended to ask Jonathan about the donkey-god later that morning, but before she could, an argument broke out between them.

Their lessons were over and Flavia had explained her plan for reuniting Vulcan and his parents.

'No, absolutely not.' Jonathan shook his head. 'It's a bad idea. And what if we're wrong?'

'But if we're right, he'll be so grateful that he'll forgive me for calling him a jackass and he'll tell us about the treasure.'

'Then you should tell him about his parents today,' said Jonathan. 'Why wait until tomorrow?'

'Because tomorrow is the Vulcanalia,' said Flavia. 'It will be perfect – just like the picture on the vase. What do *you* think, Lupus?'

Lupus scowled at Flavia.

'He doesn't like your plan because we can't tell Clio.'

'That's because she's always chattering. She wouldn't be able to keep it a secret. Besides, Rectina's her own mother and she didn't even notice the resemblance. Clio should have seen it for herself like I did.'

'You didn't figure it out,' said Jonathan. 'Lupus did!'

'I knew Rectina looked familiar,' said Flavia hotly. 'I was about to figure it out.'

'No you weren't!' said Jonathan.

'Yes I was!'

'Weren't!'

'Was!'

'You don't care about people's feelings,' said Jonathan. 'All you care about is that stupid treasure.' He stood abruptly. 'I'm going hunting. Come on Lupus!'

'I'm doing my plan whether you like it or not!' Flavia shouted after them.

'Fine! But don't expect us to help you!' The garden gate slammed behind the boys.

'Fine!' yelled Flavia, and brushed hot tears from her eyes.

The omens for the Vulcanalia were not good. Jonathan overslept and woke with a headache. Flavia and Nubia had apparently gone on ahead and the others were already leaving, so Jonathan grabbed Tigris and hurried after them through the vineyards.

It was a cool, grey morning with a sullen wind. As they crossed the coastal road and came over a rise, Jonathan saw that Titus Tascius Pomponianus and most of the inhabitants of Stabia had already gathered on the beach for the ceremony.

The most important people sat on a low wooden stage. In addition to Rectina and Tascius, who had paid for the ceremony, there were two local magistrates, a senator from Rome and Admiral Pliny. A painted wooden statue of the god Vulcan smiled down on a long brick altar covered with hot coals. Near the altar were several oak barrels. Jonathan wondered what they were for.

He looked for Flavia but couldn't see her anywhere. Then he saw Clio waving at them. She was standing with her sisters beside the platform, dressed in her favourite orange tunic. As they hurried to join her, a hush fell over the crowd. Tascius had risen and covered his head with a fold of his toga. The ceremony was about to begin. Everyone pushed closer to watch.

'Great Vulcan, god of fish and fire, anvil and anchor,' pronounced Tascius in his loudest military voice, 'be merciful this year. Protect us against the twin dangers of flame and water. And keep the grain in our warehouses from fire and damp.' The wind moaned and he raised his voice even more to be heard above it.

'Merciful Vulcan, we offer you these creatures as a living sacrifice, as substitutes for our own lives. Please accept their lives for ours. Grant that we may live another year in peace and prosperity.' Tascius paused and looked around at the crowd. Rectina smiled up at her husband and Pliny scribbled notes on his wax tablet. The crowd on the beach murmured with excitement as everyone craned for a view.

His head still covered with his toga, Tascius approached one of the oak barrels beside the platform.

'If father drops the fish, it's bad luck!' Clio whispered to Lupus and Jonathan. 'He was practising all yesterday afternoon.'

Tascius pushed the folds of his toga up over his shoulder, leaving his entire right arm bare. With a dramatic flourish he lifted his arm in the air for all to see, then plunged it into the oak cask. The crowd grew silent again. For a long moment, the only sound was the wind snapping togas and cloaks. Finally, Tascius held a live, dripping fish in the air.

'This life for my life, Great Vulcan!' he cried, and threw the fish onto the coals. The crowd cheered.

The fish, a medium-sized mackerel, thrashed for several moments and then sizzled on the red-hot coals, one eye staring glassily up at the grey sky. Jonathan stared in horrified fascination and beside him Miriam screamed and covered her eyes. Jonathan saw the fish give a few more convulsive shudders before it died.

Tascius shot Miriam a glare. Then he pulled the toga back from his head, stepped away from the barrel and turned to the crowd.

'Let us each offer a fish as substitute for our lives!' he cried. 'And let us celebrate with grain, grape and fish!'

Immediately the people on the beach surged forward and crowded round the barrels. Jonathan had to scoop up Tigris to keep him from being trampled.

Soon fish were flying through the air and dropping onto the coals. Above, seagulls circled and swooped. One bird caught a small mackerel mid-air and flew away with its prize, to the great delight of the crowd.

Some of the fish flipped out of slippery hands and fell thrashing onto the beach, only to be scooped up and thrown onto the coals, sand and all. For the sacrifice to be effective, the fish had to be alive.

Clio had just thrown her fish and now Lupus was up to his armpit in one barrel. He finally extracted a mackerel as long as his forearm. Although he could not say the words, he uttered an enthusiastic grunt as he threw the dripping creature.

'Aren't you going to sacrifice a fish, Jonathan?' laughed Clio, wiping her hands on her tunic. 'It's fun! And we get to eat them in a few minutes!'

Jonathan cradled Tigris protectively. He shook his head. 'I'm not really hungry.'

Suddenly Clio pointed up the beach.

'Here come the entertainers!' she squealed.

A fire-eater dressed in a scarlet tunic was first. He was followed by five midgets who formed a pyramid. The most popular performer was a young man dressed as the sea-nymph Thetis. He juggled four live fish while singing in a falsetto voice.

Then Jonathan heard the crowd chanting.

'Vulcan! Vul-can! Vul-*can*!'

Jonathan turned towards the coastal road. Over the dunes came a figure on a donkey. It was Vulcan the blacksmith, and on either side of him walked Flavia and Nubia.

SCROLL XX

Flavia and Nubia had hidden in the tree fort until the others left, then found Vulcan at his furnace in the tool-shed. He had mentioned earlier that he would not attend the Vulcanalia, but when Flavia told him that his long-lost parents might be on the beach, he saddled his donkey at once.

But Flavia felt uneasy.

She had envisaged a bright, sunny morning like all the other mornings so far. Vulcan and his parents would fall joyfully into each others' arms. It would be just like Vulcan's return to Mount Olympus. Then, in gratitude, he would tell her about the treasure.

Instead, the day was grey and heavy, with a peevish offshore breeze that blew fine grit and sand into their faces.

It was not a good omen.

The smell of charcoal-grilled fish and the sound of laughter reached them before they topped the sandy rise that led down to the beach.

Things seemed to improve as Vulcan came into sight. The crowd was already extremely merry due to the free wine. One or two people knew the smith's name and cried it out. Soon everyone took up the chant:

'Vulcan! Vul-can! Vul-*can*!'

As the people crowded round him, cheering and chanting his name, Vulcan smiled and looked up hopefully. Flavia's heart was pounding and she knew his must be, too. She pointed to the stage and shouted over the noise of the crowd.

'On the stage. The woman in dark blue and the man with short grey hair. No, not the stout one; that's Pliny. The tall one in the toga. Titus Tascius –'

'Pomponianus.' Vulcan's dark eyes were shining as he urged the donkey on towards the stage.

Flavia saw the crowd part before him. The faces around them were laughing and chanting Vulcan's name. Some people rose to their feet, others seemed more interested in their grilled fish.

Vulcan halted his donkey a few feet from the stage and dismounted awkwardly with the help of his staff.

Rectina had been watching his approach. When she saw the young man limping towards her, she rose unsteadily to her feet.

'Do I know you?' she asked, looking from his face to his foot and back.

But before Vulcan could answer, she fainted into her husband's arms.

'Oops,' said Flavia under her breath. 'That wasn't supposed to happen.'

Tascius, kneeling on the stage with his wife in his arms, looked up in confusion at Vulcan. 'What have you done to her? Who are you?'

'By Jove!' cried Admiral Pliny, stepping forward and peering at the blacksmith. 'It *is* him. It must be. Don't you realise who this is, Titus? It's your long-lost son!'

Tascius looked at Pliny and then back at Vulcan. A strange look passed across his face.

'My long-lost son? No, it's some sort of monstrous joke,' he said through clenched wooden teeth. 'Get him away! Get him away before she sees him again!'

The festival of Vulcan did not end well.

Everyone saw Tascius take his wife away in a curtained litter. Their daughters hurried after them on foot. Someone said Rectina had been taken ill and soon the rumour spread that she had eaten bad fish. The senator and magistrates made hasty exits, leaving Pliny to conclude the ceremony on his own.

As the admiral attempted to read out the final invocation from his notes, the crowd grew angry.

'Where's our money?'

Flavia saw Pliny consult his notes nervously and heard him ask Phrixus, 'What money? What do they want?'

'He always gives us coppers!' shrieked a woman.

'Throw coins to the crowd!' yelled another help-fully.

'By Jove,' Pliny muttered, 'I don't have any . . . I

mean . . . Phrixus, do you see a bag of coppers around here?'

One of the revellers had drunk too much free wine and he vomited noisily beside the platform.

'He's been poisoned, too!'

'It's bad luck!' someone shouted.

'Bad luck and bad fish,' said a fisherman, and spat on the sand.

'Where's our money?'

'Come on, Phrixus,' Pliny wheezed to his scribe. 'Let's get back to the ship, back to Misenum. Quickly . . .'

Flavia looked at the angry crowd and turned to Nubia. 'We'd better go, too. It might get nasty. Where's Vulcan?'

'He left just now, riding fastly his jackass.'

'You were right, Jonathan. I should have listened to you. Now I've ruined everything!'

Jonathan could see that Flavia felt miserable. They had left the angry crowd on the beach and hurried back to the farm. Now they sat at the wrought-iron table in the garden. The day was still grey and overcast, with a vicious wind that whined petulantly and rattled the leaves of the trees and shrubs.

'When a mother sees the son she thought was dead . . .' Jonathan said quietly.

'And now Vulcan's run away.'

'And you'll never find the treasure?'

'Oh Jonathan! I don't really care about the treasure. I just wanted to be able to solve the mystery for Admiral Pliny. But now he's sailed back across the bay and Vulcan has gone, too.' The moaning wind rose in volume for a moment, sounding almost angry. It whipped stinging strands of hair across Flavia's face.

'I'm sure we'll see Pliny again,' said Jonathan, patting her on the back. 'Now let's go and try to find Vulcan.'

In the middle of the night the sound of dogs barking woke Flavia from a deep sleep. She sat up, puzzled and disoriented. Then she remembered. Her plan had gone wrong. Vulcan had disappeared and they hadn't been able to find him.

Scuto's reassuring bulk was missing from the foot of her bed and Nubia's bed was empty. Flavia rose and stumbled groggily towards the sound.

She found her dog in the moon-washed farmyard. Scuto, the puppies and Ferox stood barking, their noses to the sky. The other members of the household were coming into the farmyard, holding lamps and rubbing sleep from their eyes.

The strange wind was still moaning. It blew low, fast-moving clouds across the sky towards the mountain, and the moon kept appearing and disappearing.

'You understand animals, Nubia,' whispered Flavia. 'Why are they barking?'

'The moon is not being full. I don't know.'

As her eyes adjusted to the darkness, Flavia saw a small figure shuffle out of the garden and into the farmyard. It was Frustilla. Muttering to herself, the ancient cook hobbled forward and hurled an entire bucket of cold water over the dogs.

It did the trick.

Ferox stopped barking and retreated hastily to his kennel. The other three dogs whimpered and shook themselves. Scuto trotted over to Flavia.

'What on earth has got into you, Scuto?' Flavia squatted down and ruffled the damp fur of his neck. He rolled his eyes and looked embarrassed.

'Shhh!' hissed Jonathan. Everyone was quiet.

Above moaning wind they all heard it. Faintly but unmistakably, from all the neighbouring farms and villas, the sound of dogs barking.

'Great Jupiter's eyebrows,' whispered Gaius.

And there was another sound.

'I hear squeakings,' whispered Nubia, picking up Nipur and clutching him tightly.

Lupus uttered a strangled yelp and pointed to the open garden gate. Flavia squinted. And gasped.

Emerging from beneath the myrtle and quince bushes, pattering across the mosaic walkways, skittering down the dusty paths came dozens of tiny dark shapes. There were mice, rats and even a snake.

Everyone stared as the creatures emerged from

their hiding places in house and garden, and made their way out of the garden gate and through the vineyards towards the sea.

SCROLL XXI

'I had the dream again last night.' Jonathan's face was pale and there were dark shadows under his eyes. It was a heavy, colourless dawn, the second day of the Vulcanalia. The previous day's wind had died and there was a faint, unpleasant smell in the air.

'I think the dogs must have had bad dreams, too,' said Flavia.

The puppies and Scuto lay dejectedly under a quince bush, chins on paws.

'At least they're not barking any more,' said Jonathan.

Mordecai emerged from the kitchen with a tall brass pot and seven cups on a tray. 'The well was dry this morning so I've made mint tea with yesterday's water.'

Jonathan slumped at the table.

'Have dates.' Nubia held out a plate.

'She's right,' said Aristo. 'You'll feel better when you've eaten.'

Jonathan shook his head and closed his eyes. Then he opened them again, horrified.

'Now I see it even when I close my eyes.'

'What do you see, my son?' Mordecai poured hot water onto the mint leaves.

Jonathan closed his eyes and shivered. 'I see a city on a hill, with a huge golden wall and towers. And there are legions and legions of soldiers, Roman soldiers, coming to camp around it.' He opened his eyes again. 'Something terrible is going to happen. I know it.'

'How many times have you had this dream?' asked Mordecai, gripping the back of an empty chair. In the white light of dawn his eyes seemed as black as the turban above them.

'This is the third or fourth time,' said Jonathan.

Mordecai sat heavily on the chair and stared at the steam coiling up from the cups.

'When you see Jerusalem being surrounded by armies,' he whispered, 'you will know that its desolation is near.'

'What?' Flavia frowned.

'I never said it was Jerusalem,' said Jonathan. 'I don't even know what Jerusalem looks like.'

'Yet the city you described was Jerusalem. I'm sure of it: Jerusalem the golden.' Mordecai looked at his son. 'And you *have* seen Jerusalem, you know, although you were just a baby. We were among the last people to escape before the siege began. And the fate of those left behind was truly terrible . . .'

He closed his eyes for a moment and then continued.

'I believe your dreams are from God, Jonathan.

Through you he is sending a warning to us all. The prophet in Pompeii – the one you told me about – I fear he was correct. God's judgement is about to fall upon this country.'

They all stared at him.

The sound of brass curtain rings sliding along a wooden rod cut through the heavy silence and they turned to see Miriam. She stood framed in her bedroom doorway, her cheeks wet with tears and her face as pale as marble.

'He's dead,' she whispered. 'Dead.'

'Who?' Jonathan cried. 'Who's dead?'

Miriam held up the bird cage. 'Catullus. I found him when I woke up.'

The feathered corpse of the once bright sparrow lay on the floor of the cage.

'Another portent,' said Mordecai. 'We must leave immediately. The Lord has warned us today as he once warned me, nearly ten years ago.'

In the trees above, a bird uttered a single, hesitant note, and then was silent.

Jonathan stood up and nodded. 'When I think about leaving I feel better.'

'Then pack your things. We must depart immediately.'

'No, father. I'm not going. There is no danger of besieging armies now.' Miriam had put the birdcage down. Her voice was firm.

Jonathan stared at her in amazement. Never before had he heard his sister defy their father. Her eyes were bright and a flush had crept into her pale skin.

Mordecai was staring at his daughter in disbelief.

'Miriam,' he said. 'You must come with us.'

'Father, please don't ask me to go.' The flush in her cheeks deepened. Miriam dropped her eyes and stammered, 'I want to stay here for a little longer.'

'Miriam, is there something you want to tell me?'

Again the absolute silence. Then she spoke quietly, without looking at him.

'Yes, there is. I am in love, father, and I wish to marry him. Please don't make me leave.'

'Marry? You have only just turned fourteen!'

'I'm a woman now.' Miriam lifted her eyes and looked directly at her father. 'And I'm ready to marry.'

'Yes. I suppose you are.' Mordecai's voice was barely more than a whisper. 'Well, who is it? Whom do you love?'

'She is in love with me,' came a voice from beneath the peristyle. 'And I would give my life for her.'

SCROLL XXII

The man who emerged from the house and stepped into the garden was the last person Flavia expected. She gasped:

'Uncle Gaius!'

Lupus choked in amazement and Jonathan's jaw dropped. Only Nubia seemed to accept this revelation calmly.

To Flavia, it seemed unbelievable. How could Jonathan's sister want to marry a man her father's age? But when he and Miriam looked at one another, Flavia saw the love in their eyes.

Mordecai's face softened. 'Then you must come with us, too, Gaius. We must all leave Italia. And quickly, I beg of you. We can discuss this matter later.'

Gaius took a few steps towards Mordecai and held his hands out, palms to the sky. 'But how? How can I leave my villa, my vines, the farm? If there's another strong earthquake I have to stay here to protect the house against looters and thieves. If I must face God's judgement, then I would rather face it here in the house where I was born.'

'No. Father's right.' Jonathan looked around at them all. 'We have to leave! Don't you understand?'

Mordecai nodded. 'Nearly ten years ago, when I saw Jerusalem beginning to be surrounded by armies, I remembered the words of the Shepherd: "Let those who are in Judaea flee to the mountains. Let no one on the roof of his house go down to take anything out of the house. Let no one in the field go back to get his cloak. For then there will be great distress, not seen from the beginning of the world until now."

'I felt a sense of dread then, just as Jonathan does now. And it was that sense of dread which saved our lives. My children and I left Jerusalem immediately. But their mother . . . their mother . . .'

To Flavia's dismay, Mordecai began to weep.

'She was so beautiful,' he said, and turned to Miriam. 'So much like you, my dear. She refused to go, just as you are refusing to go. We argued, and she decided to stay with her parents. I relented and I never saw her again.'

Mordecai held out his hands to his daughter.

'Miriam. What good is a warning from the Lord if we refuse to listen? You must come with us.'

Before Miriam could reply, something soft struck Flavia's bare arm.

'Oh!' she cried. A wren lay at her feet in the dust.

Flavia bent down and gently picked it up. 'I think it's dead,' she said. 'But it's still warm.' She looked up into the leaves of the laurel tree, just in time to see three more birds drop from its branches.

Suddenly all around them the trees were raining birds: a shower of wrens, thrushes and sparrows. Nubia knelt to pick up a tiny sparrow.

'Birds dead,' she whispered. 'All dead.'

'What on earth . . .' said Aristo, staring at the feathered corpses around them.

'Rotten eggs!' cried Gaius. 'I should have remembered!'

'You should have remembered what?' asked Flavia.

'Sulphur smells like rotten eggs,' said her uncle, 'and sulphur fumes are what killed the sheep up near Misenum in the big earthquake seventeen years ago.'

Flavia sniffed the air. There was a distinct scent of rotten eggs.

'But if the smell of sulphur can kill animals as large as sheep . . .' said Aristo. He didn't need to finish the sentence.

As they stood staring at each other, a voice broke the silence.

'My mother always told me that the smell of rotten eggs meant that Vulcan was angry.'

They all turned to see Frustilla standing in the kitchen doorway.

'My grandmother was from the island of Sicily,' quavered the old woman, shuffling into the garden, 'where the smith god has his forge . . .'

'And when the smith god is angry –' said Jonathan.

'There's a volcano!' cried Flavia.

As if to confirm Flavia's words, the ground rumbled beneath their feet, and they heard a sound like distant thunder.

'Of course,' said Mordecai. 'I should have guessed! You're right, Miriam. There are no besieging armies. This time God's judgement will come by natural disaster. He has been warning those of us with eyes to see. The sulphur, the tremors, dry wells, the odd behaviour of the animals, Jonathan's dreams . . . Frustilla is right. They all point to one thing: a volcanic eruption.'

'But which mountain will erupt?' asked Jonathan.

'It has to be Vesuvius!' cried Aristo.

'But it's not a volcano. It's never erupted,' said Gaius. 'Has it, Frustilla?'

'Not in my lifetime,' said the old cook. 'And I've never heard of it being a fire-spitter. But there's a small volcano north of it, near Misenum. They say it smells of rotten eggs.'

'Vesuvius could be dormant . . . that is, a sleeping volcano . . .' Mordecai tugged his beard. 'I believe I know how we can find out! Gaius, do you have Pliny's *Natural History*? I'm certain there is a section on volcanoes . . .'

'There's a copy in the library,' answered Gaius.

They all hurried into the library and Flavia's uncle lifted down a fat cylindrical scroll-case marked 'Pliny'.

'Quickly!' said Flavia, hopping with impatience. 'I think there's something about Vesuvius in scroll three!'

Miriam gently pushed Gaius's fumbling hand away and swiftly unpicked the cord with her deft fingers. Together they eased off the leather lid.

Meanwhile, Aristo had moved to a dim corner of the library. He was passing a clay lamp along the wall and peering at the dangling leather labels.

For several moments the only sound was the crackle and rustle of papyrus scrolls being unrolled on the library table.

'Here's something about Vesuvius!' cried Flavia at last. She scanned the passage. 'But Pliny doesn't say anything about it being a volcano.'

In his shadowy corner, Aristo pulled a scroll from its niche.

'Listen to this!' said Jonathan. 'In scroll two, Pliny lists some volcanoes around the world. He doesn't mention Vesuvius, but he says that there is a small fire in Modena that erupts every year on the feast day of Vulcan. That's now!'

Gaius shook his head. 'Modena is as far north of Rome as we are south of it.'

'Eureka!' cried Aristo from his corner. 'I've found it!'

He moved over to the doorway, set down his lamp and unrolled a scroll.

'Diodorus of Sicily tells about strange animal

behaviour several centuries ago near my home town in Greece. I'd forgotten the exact details, but here it is!'

He read aloud. ' "In a town called Helice on the gulf of Corinth, there was a devastating earthquake. Before the earthquake struck, to the puzzlement of the citizens, all sorts of animals, such as rats, snakes and weasels, left the city in droves." '

'Exactly like last night,' said Jonathan.

Aristo was silent for a moment as he scanned the text. Then the colour drained from his face.

'What?' They all gazed at him anxiously.

' "Five days later",' he read, ' "the entire town was swallowed up by the sea." '

SCROLL XXIII

There was a long silence as they all looked at one another, broken only by Ferox barking in the farmyard.

'We must warn people,' said Mordecai, after a moment. 'I'm a fool. The Lord has been trying to tell us for days, but I didn't see the signs.'

'Neither did Pliny,' said Flavia, 'and he is the greatest natural historian in the world.'

'Do we escape by land or by sea?' said Aristo.

'The quickest route is always by sea,' Mordecai said. 'But we must escape any way we can . . .'

Suddenly the garden gate swung open.

'Vulcan!' cried Flavia.

'Clio!' said Jonathan.

'Modestus!' said Nubia.

The muscular blacksmith and the little girl in the orange tunic stood side by side, with the donkey's big head nosing between them.

Lupus ran to Clio and stopped shyly in front of her. Her face was blotched and tear-stained, but she smiled back at him.

'Vulcan, where were you?' Flavia asked. 'We looked everywhere for you.'

'I rode south,' he said. 'Modestus and I slept on the beach. Just now I presented myself at the Villa Pomponiana, but Tascius refused to see me and Rectina wasn't there. On my way back here I found Clio.'

Mordecai stepped forward. 'Listen to me. We believe Vesuvius is going to erupt and that we must get as far away from it as we can.'

'The best route of escape is probably by sea,' added Gaius. 'Clio, you're lucky your family has a boat. You must all sail away as soon as you can.'

'But –'

'You must get out as soon as possible!' urged Mordecai. 'All of you!'

'We can't.' Clio's eyes filled with tears. 'Mother and Father had a horrible argument last night. Mother took my sisters and three slaves and she left for her villa at dawn. I jumped off the back of the carruca and came back to find out why, because Mother wouldn't tell us anything.' Tears ran down Clio's face. Lupus offered her a grubby handkerchief.

'Please, Clio,' said Mordecai. 'Try to be calm. Tell us again: where is your mother's villa?'

'Just the other side of Herculaneum,' said Clio, blowing her nose on Lupus's scrap of linen. 'Two miles north of the Neapolis gate.'

'Great Jupiter's eyebrows!' said Gaius. 'It's at the very foot of the mountain!'

Even as he spoke, the earth trembled and shook beneath them once more.

*

'We must warn those beneath the mountain,' said Flavia's uncle grimly.

He ran his hand through his hair just as Flavia's father did when he was upset. 'I'll go to Pompeii immediately and tell the authorities what we've discovered. Then I'll ride inland to Nuceria and warn them, too. But someone will have to go to Oplontis and Herculaneum, and then on to Neapolis . . .'

'I will,' said Vulcan without hesitation. 'It may be the last chance I get to see . . . my mother.'

'Are you sure?' asked Mordecai. 'You may be riding to your death.'

'Deaths holds no fear for me,' said Vulcan bravely, and then swallowed. 'Well, only a little.'

'I know you can ride a donkey,' said Gaius. 'But can you ride a fast horse?'

Vulcan nodded.

'Good,' said Gaius. 'Then we must leave immediately.'

'I'll go too, if you need me.' Aristo stepped forward.

Gaius smiled. 'Thank you Aristo, but I need you and Mordecai to get my household to safety. Tell Xanthus to harness the mules to the carriage. Vulcan and I will take Celer and Audax.' He turned to the doctor.

'Mordecai, can you drive a carriage?'

'Yes, of course.'

'Will you drive Miriam and the children to Stabia? Take Frustilla, too, and Rufus. Drop Clio home on your way. Aristo, will you and Xanthus follow on foot with my other slaves? When you all get to Stabia, board a ship and sail away from here as soon as you can. I'll give you all the gold in my strongbox.'

'You don't have to go to Stabia,' sniffed Clio. 'Our boat is big enough for you all. Father will take you.'

'Are you sure?'

Clio nodded.

'Excellent,' Gaius said. 'Mordecai. Aristo. Get everyone to the Villa Pomponiana and sail as soon as you can. Don't wait for us.'

Suddenly Miriam threw her arms around Gaius. 'Don't go! Stay with us!'

'I must go, my darling,' said Gaius, softly, and brushed dark curls away from her face. 'How could you still love me if I didn't try to help all the people whose lives are in danger?'

'But what if you're wrong? What if it's all a mistake? What if they are just tremors?'

'Then no harm will come to us. Except perhaps from angry citizens.'

'But, Gaius –'

'Shhh!' he whispered. 'I've waited all my life for you and I'm not about to lose you now. I promise I'll return.'

As they embraced, Aristo and Vulcan glanced at each other.

'I gave her the bracelet,' confessed Vulcan. 'I made it myself.'

'I gave her the sparrow,' Aristo said.

Vulcan frowned. 'Then that means he –'

'*He* didn't give her anything,' said Aristo with a sigh.

At two hours past dawn, Vulcan and Gaius rode out of the farmyard to warn the towns near Vesuvius of the coming disaster.

Vulcan planned to tell the town magistrates of Oplontis, Herculaneum and Neapolis.

Gaius was heading for Pompeii and then Nuceria. Ferox, freed from his hated kennel, ran joyfully beside his master. He easily kept up with the galloping horses. As soon as they were out of sight, Mordecai turned to the children.

'I'll give you half an hour to pack your things. Take only what you can carry. And hurry. I feel in my spirit that disaster is almost upon us.'

Flavia and Nubia had just finished packing when they heard Mordecai shouting. For a moment they stared at one another. They had never before heard his voice raised in anger.

'I couldn't stop him, father!' Jonathan cried.

The girls hurried out of their bedroom and into the garden. Jonathan and his father stood face to face.

'But why didn't you tell me immediately?' The

anger in Mordecai's voice made his accent more pronounced.

'He made me promise.' Jonathan looked miserable.

'And Clio's with him?'

'No. *He's* with *her*. She's the one who insisted on going. He told me – I mean he let me know – that he was only going along to protect her.'

'Those two are the most stubborn, rebellious souls I've ever met,' said Mordecai. 'They're just the same!'

He noticed Aristo and the girls watching him open-mouthed.

'Lupus and Clio have taken – no, *stolen* one of the horses. Clio's gone after Vulcan to try to save her family. Of all the foolish . . . Lupus the eight-year-old has gone to protect Clio the seven-year-old. Dear Lord!' He looked up into the sky. 'What else could possibly go wrong?'

The garden gate opened and Xanthus staggered in. He was bloody and beaten, his clothing ripped and torn.

'The slaves,' he gasped. 'I tried to stop them but they've all run away. And they've taken the mules and carriage.'

SCROLL XXIV

Lupus and Clio had hoped to catch up with Vulcan on the road to Pompeii, but they were not the only ones to have a premonition of disaster. A steady stream of people moving against them made it difficult to travel quickly.

'Go back!' one or two travellers shouted at them. 'The god Vulcan has just told us that there's a furnace beneath Vesuvius. It's about to explode.'

'At least we're on the right track,' said Clio over her shoulder to Lupus.

Lupus grunted in response. He wasn't used to riding. Already his bottom ached from half an hour of bouncing.

At the harbour of Pompeii, half the ships were gone and scores of people were trying to board those that remained. Women and children were screaming and men were fighting. There was a sinister red stain on the pavement in front of the tavern with the yellow awning.

Passing between the harbour and the town walls, Lupus and Clio saw an official standing beneath the arch of the Sea Gate.

'By order of the magistrate,' he shouted, 'do not leave the city. The tremors are not dangerous! Stay in your homes, or they may be looted! Return to your homes immediately, I say!'

A few people hesitated when they heard his words, but most kept their heads down as they hurried past him through the gate.

'I thought Flavia's uncle was going to tell them about the mountain,' said Clio.

Lupus grunted yes.

'Then I don't understand why that man in the toga is telling people not to leave.'

At first sight, the Villa Pomponiana seemed deserted. It was now late morning, baking hot, with only a breath of wind from the bay.

Jonathan was sweating as he and Flavia helped Mordecai lift Xanthus off Modestus. Nubia led the donkey across to the stables while they carried Xanthus up the steps to the dining-room and eased him onto a dining couch. The farm manager's broken ankle and ribs would mend, but his punctured lung was grave.

Aristo had been carrying old Frustilla on his back. As soon as he set her down she and Miriam went off to find a basin and water so that Mordecai could treat Xanthus.

'Find Tascius, if you can,' said Mordecai, glancing up at Jonathan and Flavia.

They nodded and ran through the silent rooms and inner courtyards.

At last they found Tascius in the atrium, hunched in front of the household shrine. He heard them enter, and lifted his head from his hands.

'They've all left me. My wife, my daughters, most of my slaves. Not even a live chicken to sacrifice to the gods.'

'We've got to get away from here,' said Jonathan. 'Something terrible is going to happen. We think Vesuvius is going to erupt. Flavia's Uncle Gaius and Vulcan have gone to warn people in the towns.'

Tascius looked at them stupidly.

'Vesuvius is a volcano,' said Flavia. 'It's going to erupt!'

'When? How?'

'Soon! I mean, we don't know exactly,' said Jonathan, 'but we must leave!'

'If you're right . . . Jupiter! My wife and daughters are in Herculaneum.'

'Can't we rescue them in your boat?' asked Flavia.

Tascius shook his head. 'Could have yesterday, when the wind was from the south. But not today. Can't even sail out of Stabia today.'

It was almost noon when Clio and Lupus rode their horse through the bright, sunny streets of Herculaneum. It was a smaller, prettier town than Pompeii, with red roofs and palm trees, but it seemed all the more vulnerable because of the huge mountain which loomed above it, filling half the sky.

'Until last year, we used to live here,' Clio said, looking around. 'I've never seen it so quiet.'

As they passed a tavern, two drunks called out from the shady doorway.

'Hey! Haven't you heard? The god Vulcan passed by earlier and told everyone to flee the city. And they all believed him. All except for us! We get free wine!'

His companion snorted. 'Ha! "Vulcan" is probably going through their money boxes right now.' He drained his wine-cup and stepped outside the tavern. 'Nice-looking horse . . . Want us to take her off your hands?' He nodded at his companion and the two of them lurched towards the children.

Clio stuck out her tongue at the men and kicked her heels. The tired mare trotted down the hill and out through the Neapolis Gate.

In the dining-room of the Villa Pomponiana, Nubia shivered and hugged Nipur tightly.

It was just past midday and she stood beside Flavia watching Mordecai try to save the farm manager's life. Xanthus had suddenly begun to cough blood and seemed unable to breathe. His face was a horrible blue colour. Nubia saw tiny beads of sweat on Mordecai's forehead as he and Miriam tried to staunch the flow of blood.

A moment earlier, the noonday heat had been stifling. Now the air around her was freezing cold.

Nubia shivered again.

She had felt this presence once before.

The day the slave-traders had burnt her family's tents and murdered her father. Was the presence death? Or something worse?

The floor vibrated under Nubia's feet, like one of Scuto's silent growls. The earth itself was angry, but no one else seemed to notice.

Nubia glanced back over her shoulder towards Vesuvius. And froze.

An enormous white column was rising from the mountain's peak.

The fact that it was rising in complete silence made it all the more terrifying.

Lupus hit the ground with a force that knocked the breath out of him. He was dimly aware of Clio beside him and the mare's bulk above them, blocking out the sunlight as she reared. For an awful moment he thought the falling horse would crush them both.

Then, with a scream of terror, the mare found her balance and galloped off towards the south.

Lupus had still not managed to get air back into his lungs. Finally it came in a great sobbing breath. Clio's body beside him remained terribly still.

He heard thunder and felt the ground shudder

beneath him. Then Lupus saw what had terrified the horse.

Rising straight into the air from the mountain above him was a huge pillar of white smoke and ash.

Vesuvius was erupting, and he was at its very base!

SCROLL XXV

The thunder continued, rumbling up from the earth itself. Bits of gravel and tiny fragments of hot pumice began to rain down on Lupus.

Ignoring this stinging hail, he shook Clio and patted her cheeks. He tried to call her name, but the only sound that came from his mouth was an animal-like groan.

Lupus had never wanted his tongue back so badly. He wanted it back so that he could curse every god who existed.

But he didn't have a tongue and he couldn't curse the gods, even though Clio was dead.

The sound of the volcano reached Stabia a moment after Jonathan watched his father stab Xanthus.

The farm manager had been raving, calling out to the gods. Grimly, Mordecai had told Miriam to get the long needle from his capsa. She had reached into the cylindrical leather case and pulled out a long, wickedly sharp knife.

They stared in horrified fascination at Xanthus's blue, gasping face. Mordecai ripped open the injured man's tunic, fixed the point of the needle at his side between two ribs and pushed. There was a sound like air escaping as the needle pierced the dying man's lung. Then Xanthus gasped and his chest seemed to swell. The colour began to return to his face.

'Thank God,' whispered Mordecai. 'Miriam, make a poultice to seal –'

At that moment the sound of deep thunder reached them. They all turned to look behind them.

'Oh no,' said Jonathan.

'Dear Apollo' Aristo said.

'Not now!' cried Mordecai. 'Not now!'

The thick column above the cone of Vesuvius, white against the brilliant blue sky, was already beginning to blossom.

Even as they watched, the top of the cloud spread and flattened, until it had taken the shape of an enormous umbrella pine.

The mountain had been thundering for an eternity.

He had been carrying her body forever. Chips of hot pumice and grit spattered him like hail, so that there were a hundred tiny cuts and burns on his arms and legs and face.

Sometimes he fell and sobbed, then he picked her up again and continued up the dirt path between black, flame-shaped cypress trees. If there was a place reserved in the afterlife to punish the wicked, this was it. He knew he had failed and deserved no less.

And so he carried her on up the path to the smoking villa and the waiting god, who stood staring at him in disbelief and amazement. Truly the smith god, whose dwelling place was beneath the earth in darkness and fire, must be king of this realm, and so he handed the little girl's body to Vulcan.

Then Lupus fainted.

Tascius stumbled down the steps and stood in the middle of the green lawn, staring at the volcano with his arms outstretched.

'The gods!' he cried. 'They can't bear our evil any more. They can't bear *my* evil. It's Vulcan. It's Vulcan's anger. The gods tested me and I failed.' He fell to his knees on the grass and began to scratch his cheeks.

The others looked at him aghast.

After a moment, Mordecai left Xanthus and went down the steps and into the hot sunlight. He tried to help Tascius to his feet.

'Tascius,' he said firmly, 'you are a Roman soldier and commander. You must take charge. You must get the household on board your boat and prepare to sail as soon as the wind shifts.'

'It's no use!' Tascius pointed at the volcano. 'Vulcan's anger has come upon me and I must die.' He grasped his own tunic and ripped it at the neck.

'Titus Tascius Pomponianus!' cried Mordecai, gripping the Roman's wrists, 'If it is indeed time for you to die, let your death be honourable. Set an example to these young people.'

They stared into each other's eyes for a long moment.

'Yes,' said Tascius at last, taking a deep breath and nodding his head. 'The gods may have taken everything else, but they cannot take my dignity. Not unless I allow it.' Slowly the old soldier rose to his feet. 'You are right, doctor. I'll prepare the boat at once.'

Someone was pouring cool water down Lupus's scorched throat. It went down the wrong way and he had to sit up to cough.

When he had caught his breath, he opened his eyes. Vulcan stood over him, with Rectina close beside him. Their brown eyes, so similar, were filled with tenderness and concern.

One of Clio's younger sisters, Urania, was clinging to Rectina's skirts. Thalia hovered nearby, her face swollen and blotched with weeping. Lupus was aware of a thunder in his ears and a sound like hail on the roof.

Rectina held the beaker out again and Lupus drained it.

'How did you find us?' asked Vulcan when Lupus had finished. 'God must have guided you.'

Lupus snarled and gave the rudest gesture he knew. He meant it for the gods, but Vulcan recoiled as if he had been struck. Then he swallowed.

'You have been through terrible things, Lupus. We all have. Don't be afraid.'

Lupus wanted to explain that he wasn't afraid – he was furious. But he couldn't, so he lay back on the couch and closed his eyes. The house rattled around them as if it were a moving carriage.

Lupus felt a cool, moist sea sponge on his forehead and he heard Rectina's gentle voice.

'Thank you for bringing my little Clio back to me, Lupus,' she said. 'At first we feared she was dead, but when Vulcan laid his hands on her and prayed –'

Lupus was off the couch in an instant. He pushed past Rectina and Vulcan and looked frantically around. He stood in the middle of an elegant red and black atrium, with chairs and couches and easy access to the garden, but he saw none of it.

All he saw was Clio in her grubby orange tunic, sitting on the couch opposite him, smiling weakly. She was pale and dishevelled, but she was very much alive.

SCROLL XXVI

'My boat's ready to sail,' said Tascius, coming up the steps from the direction of the beach. 'Packed and provisioned with food and water.' He wiped his forehead with the back of his forearm.

'Most of my slaves have gone. I've posted the remaining few to guard the boat. Promised them a passage to safety and their freedom as a reward.' He slumped into a chair and turned his face towards Vesuvius.

Jonathan looked round at the others. 'If the boat's ready, shouldn't we go?'

'Wind's still against us,' said Tascius. 'Stronger now, too.'

'Maybe we could go to the harbour of Stabia and hire a boat there,' Jonathan persisted.

'They're at the mercy of the wind, just as we are. The only boats which might escape are small rowing boats or the big oared warships.'

'Couldn't we go in a carriage?' suggested Flavia. She had her arm around a whimpering Scuto and was trying to soothe him.

'Rectina has taken it,' said Tascius. 'I have a small cart and a chariot. But they're of no use.'

'Then we should walk.' Jonathan was finding it hard to breathe, but it was not the asthma that pressed hard on his chest. It was fear.

'We can sail as far in one hour as we could walk in twelve,' said Tascius, and then added, 'if the wind shifts.'

'But what if the wind doesn't shift?' asked Jonathan.

'A gamble we'll have to take.'

'Father!' cried Jonathan in desperation.

Mordecai looked up from the couch. 'I'm sorry, Jonathan. This man can't be moved and if I leave him he'll die.'

'Then so will we,' said Jonathan bleakly.

'Lupus,' said Vulcan, raising his voice to be heard above the volcano's thunder. 'We need your help.'

Lupus looked up at him and nodded. He sat beside Clio, with his arm protectively round her shoulders, still amazed by what had happened to her. Had she just been unconscious? He was certain she had died.

'Lupus? Are you listening? Good. The road north has just been blocked by a landslide and my mother's only sailing boat has been stolen. We're trapped at the foot of a volcano.'

A sharp cracking sound cut through the steady background rumble and they all paused as the house shuddered. A marble statue in the garden toppled forward and crashed to the ground.

'My mother has an idea,' continued Vulcan. 'It's our

one chance of escape. If we can get a message to Admiral Pliny across the bay, he might send war ships to rescue not just us, but all the others trapped here at the foot of the volcano. My mother is writing the message now.'

Lupus made a gesture with his palms up and grunted. The sense was clear: 'How?'

'Rectina has a small rowing boat in the boathouse down by the shore,' said Vulcan. 'I can row, but because of my foot I cannot run. When we reach Misenum, someone will have to take the message quickly to the admiral. Clio says you are fast and brave. Also, you know what Pliny looks like.'

A shower of gravel and pumice fragments rattled on the roof above them.

'I wanted to go,' said Clio. 'But they say I'm too weak. You'll go, won't you?'

Without hesitation, Lupus nodded.

'Good,' said Rectina, coming into the room. She staggered a little, for the earth was still vibrating beneath them. 'I've just finished writing this message. Pliny will not refuse me. He is a brave man.'

She handed Lupus an oilskin packet about the size of his thumb. It had been tied with leather cords, dipped in liquid wax and sealed with her signet ring, the coiling hearth-snake of good fortune.

'When you get to Misenum,' Rectina said, 'you must run as fast as you can to the admiral's house. It's at the very top of the hill. Three enormous poplar trees stand beside the entrance. Do you understand, Lupus? Vulcan will row. And you will run.' She kissed his forehead. 'May the gods protect you.'

At the Villa Pomponiana, they stared across the bay towards the mountain, praying for the wind to change. But the cloud of ash above Vesuvius was unfurling to the south and they could see their prayers had not yet been answered.

Presently, while Mordecai and Miriam quietly worked to keep Xanthus breathing, Tascius told them the true story of Vulcan's birth.

'I first met Pliny when he was a guest in this very house,' Tascius began, pouring himself a cup of wine.

'He served with my father in Germania. They grew close on campaign. Pliny was very like my father. A brilliant scholar as well as a man of action. I was a good soldier, but not clever. Pliny was the man my father always hoped I would be.'

He paused and looked around at them. Beneath the solid line of his eyebrows his eyes looked bruised.

'I've never spoken of this to anyone. Look who I'm telling now. Jews, slaves and children.' He made a dismissive gesture. 'Doesn't matter. I'll be dead soon.'

He took a sip of wine.

'When Rectina and I were first married, she lived here. With my parents. I was away on campaign most of the time. That was when Pliny came here as a guest, to finish his biography of my father. Pliny is old and stout now like me. But eighteen years ago he was in his prime.'

Tascius paused and stared into his wine-cup, as if he could see the past reflected in the dark liquid.

'I was often away. Pliny was always here. With my father. And with Rectina. Once I caught them speaking together, laughing. That was when I first suspected.'

'Nine months later, after Pliny went back to his dusty scrolls, Rectina gave birth to a son. A son born with a mark of the gods' disapproval. A clubfoot.'

'Do you mean . . . ?' Flavia gasped as she realised what Tascius was saying.

'Yes,' said Tascius. 'Vulcan is not my son. He is Pliny's!'

SCROLL XXVII

In a small rowing boat on the vast bay of Neapolis, Lupus watched the blacksmith in awe. Vulcan had been rowing for nearly an hour. He had only paused twice: first to shrug off the cloak meant to protect him from the rain of gravel and ash, and later to strip off even his tunic. Now he sat in a loincloth, his powerful chest and arms dripping with sweat. The veins stood out on his arms and hands, pumping blood to muscles that must be screaming with pain.

The blacksmith's gentle face was frozen in a grimace. It was bloody and blackened with a hundred tiny cuts and scorches. His lips were cracked and dry. Lupus knew that ashes had burnt the inside of Vulcan's mouth, as they had his, and that it must be agony for him to swallow.

Lupus took a swig from the water gourd Rectina had given them and then offered it to the smith.

His teeth bared, Vulcan shook his head and continued to pull with every fibre of his being towards Misenum, still four miles distant.

*

'Does Vulcan know that Pliny is his father?' asked Flavia.

Tascius shook his head. 'I don't believe he does know. Unless of course he's reached Rectina at Herculaneum and she's told him.'

He gazed towards the blue bay and the volcano beyond. The tree-shaped pillar of ash which rose from Vesuvius was no longer white but a dirty grey. The ground still trembled beneath them.

'I suspected Rectina was pregnant with Pliny's baby. When he was born, I saw the clubfoot. That was when I knew he wasn't mine.' He drained his cup again. 'I named him Publius.' Tascius gave a hollow laugh. 'After my father.'

'Did you ever tell your wife what you suspected?' asked Aristo.

Tascius shook his head. 'I didn't want to lose her. I loved her, you see. Later I couldn't accuse her because . . .' Tascius refilled his cup with undiluted wine.

'The world will soon end. May as well tell you everything.

'Soon after the baby was born, I'd finished my military service. We decided to move to Rectina's Herculaneum villa. Only took two slaves with us. The rest were due to arrive in a day or two, with our belongings. It was a tiring journey. Rectina went to have a nap with the baby.

'Somehow I found myself in Rectina's room. The

baby lay next to her on the couch. I remember he was wrapped up tightly in swaddling clothes. I picked him up. He opened his eyes. Great dark eyes like Rectina's.

'I carried him to the window. A low window with iron bars. Overlooking vineyards. I rested the baby on the sill against the bars. Then I went outside.'

Tascius got up from his couch and stood near the colonnade, where the shade ended and the sunshine began. His back was to them now but they could still hear his voice.

'If the baby had cried, or made the slightest noise. But he didn't. From outside the window it was easy enough to pull him through the bars.

'I saddled a horse. Rode to Pompeii and left him in some bushes by the river. Slave-girls were washing their clothes nearby. He began to cry as I rode off. I knew he would be found.'

Tascius paused for a moment, resting his head against one of the cool white columns.

'On my way back to the villa, I stopped at Herculaneum to see an old friend. In case anyone should ask where I'd been. Had a cup of wine with him. When I returned at dusk, the house was in uproar. Rectina was . . . I thought she might be relieved to be rid of the baby. But her anguish was terrible. I never wanted to hurt her.'

There was a distant rumble from the volcano and another tremor shook the villa. Tascius's wine-cup, which he had left near the edge of the table, fell and shattered on the marble floor. Tascius did not turn around and no one else moved.

'The next morning I rode back to Pompeii. Searched the river bank. Made enquiries. Posted rewards. Punished our house-slaves. But the baby had vanished.

'Later, I thought that if Rectina had another child perhaps she would forget the first one. But there were no more babies. Rectina's womb had closed up with grief. Or perhaps the gods were punishing me.' He turned and looked at them.

'When Rectina took in that first little orphan girl, she seemed happy again. I allowed her to keep the baby. And eventually eight more. You've seen how I love them. How much they love me. I'm a good father.' His face relaxed for a moment. Then he frowned and walked over to the shattered wine-cup. He knelt beside it and began picking up the shards of clay.

'Then when *he* appeared at the Vulcanalia yesterday, she fainted. I brought her back here. When she revived she desperately wanted to know where he was. I told her I didn't know. She looked at me and said "It was our son, wasn't it, Titus?" and I said "Not our son, *your* son." She asked what I meant. At last I said what I had never said before: "That cripple was never mine. He was Pliny's child." She looked at me. And I think . . . For the first time she realised what I had done all those years ago.'

Tascius stood and squeezed his thumb where he had pricked it on one of the shards.

His voice faltered. 'Then Rectina asked me where he was. And may the gods forgive me. I said . . . I said, "Who? Pliny, or your son?" '

Tascius looked at the drop of red blood on his thumb.

'Early this morning she took my daughters and left me forever. Now I am truly alone.'

Lupus and Vulcan were less than two miles from Misenum, with the harbour in clear sight, when something struck the blacksmith's forehead and knocked him backwards.

At first Lupus thought Vulcan was dead. He crawled forward and pressed his fingertips against Vulcan's neck, as he had once seen Mordecai do. After a moment he felt a pulse, weak but steady.

As he took his hand away, Lupus noticed his fingertips were covered in blood. The blow had left an ugly gash at Vulcan's hairline. He found the still smoking pumice and weighed it in his hand. It was an ugly chunk of rock, denser and heavier than the pumice which had fallen so far. It must have struck Vulcan a glancing blow. A direct hit would surely have killed him.

Lupus stood up, planted his feet apart to stop the boat from rocking and calculated the distance to the harbour. A mile. A mile and a half at most. He could try to row but first he would have to shift Vulcan's powerful body and that would take too long.

It would be quicker to swim. He had covered that distance a month before, but he had been strong then and it had been a fine, fair day.

Now the sky was raining ash and gravel. And ugly lumps of clay mixed with pumice, like the one that had struck Vulcan. Lupus fingered the oilcloth pouch around his neck, Rectina's message to Pliny. He knew it was the only hope for Clio and her sisters.

He stripped off his tunic, took a deep breath and jumped.

SCROLL XXVIII

As Lupus plunged into the bay he almost cried out. The salt water made every tiny cut and burn on his face and body sting. It felt as if a hundred needles were pricking his skin.

He knew salt water was good for surface wounds. He had heard Doctor Mordecai telling one of his patients, a man with sores on his skin, to bathe in the sea.

But this water had a scum of ash floating on its surface and his back was exposed to a steady rain of debris from the volcano.

Soon, Lupus began to tire. He had been up since before dawn, had ridden for two hours, had carried Clio at least half a mile. Now his arms ached and his lungs could not take in enough air.

He stopped to tread water for a moment. He could see a man-made breakwater no more than half a mile distant and beyond it the masts which marked the naval port. He could even make out the silhouette of three poplars on one of the hills overlooking the harbour. Those three trees marked his goal, the admiral's home.

Hundreds, maybe thousands of lives, depended on him. He took a breath and struck out again.

'Here! Give me your hand, boy. Up you come. By Hercules! What have you done to yourself? And what were you doing paddling about among the Roman fleet? This is a restricted area, you know. Soldiers and marines only. Caius! Have you got a blanket? An old cloak? Anything? Yes, that'll do. Wrap this round yourself, boy. Better? Now under ordinary circumstances I'd have to report you to – Hey! Where are you going? Come back, you mongrel! That's not your cloak!'

At the Villa Pomponiana in Stabia, Nubia ran to one of the dining-room columns.

'Bug-boats!' She cried and pointed towards the bay. From beneath a couch, Nipur sensed her excitement and began to bark.

'Bug-boats?' said Tascius, frowning at the slave-girl.

'There!' cried Jonathan. 'Coming out from behind the promontory. Warships! One, two, three, four . . .'

'By the gods, you have good eyesight.' Tascius squinted. 'Yes . . . yes! I see them. Looks like the imperial fleet!'

'Those ships are powered by oar, are they not?' asked Aristo.

'Yes,' replied Tascius, 'by both oar and sail.'

'Then they can go anywhere, even against the wind.'

'But where *are* they going?' asked Jonathan.

'I'd guess Herculaneum,' said Tascius.

'It's the admiral!' cried Flavia, jumping to her feet and clapping her hands. 'It's Admiral Pliny! He's launched the imperial Roman fleet to rescue the people at the foot of the volcano!'

Jonathan added, 'And please, God, to rescue us, too!'

Lupus sat on a couch in the warship's open cabin, wearing an oversized tunic and sipping warm honeyed wine. The sleek warship sped over the water, its banks of oars rising and falling in time to the rowers' chant. Behind them followed a dozen similar warships.

Admiral Pliny reclined beside Lupus. In his hand was Rectina's note. The admiral had read it several times but now he unfolded the papyrus again. Pliny's scribe Phrixus stood nearby, his stylus poised over a wax tablet.

'She writes that she is terrified by the danger threatening her and she begs me to rescue her and her daughters from an awful fate . . .' Pliny read it aloud and then looked down at Lupus. 'It's a good thing you came when you did. Phrixus and I were just about to take a much smaller boat to investigate the phenomenon. I had no idea the volcano posed such a threat to the inhabitants.'

As they passed the promontory of Puteoli, Lupus thought of Vulcan, lying unconscious in a rowing boat. He stood and gazed over the water, then grunted and pointed to his right.

'What is it? What do you see?'

Lupus walked back and forth in front of the admiral, imitating Vulcan's limp.

'Have you injured your foot? Are you hurt?'

Lupus shook his head vigorously, then snatched the wax tablet from the scribe's startled hands. Phrixus uttered an exclamation, but Pliny held up his hand. They both watched as the boy wrote something in the wax.

Lupus had been studying with Aristo for over a month and he had learned his alphabet and a few basic words. He had never written the name Vulcan before, but now he tried, sounding out each letter in his head as Aristo had taught him. Then he handed the tablet to Pliny. On it he had written in neat capitals:

VOLCAN

'Yes, my boy, very astute! The phenomenon we are witnessing is indeed a "volcano". I never suspected that Vesuvius –'

Lupus snatched the tablet back from the startled admiral and added two words. He showed Pliny the tablet again.

VOLCAN IN A BOAT

Then he pointed out to sea.

'Over there!' cried Phrixus. 'I see something. A small rowing boat! The blacksmith Vulcan must be in that boat.'

SCROLL XXIX

Flavia helped Jonathan tie a linen napkin over the lower half of his face. He had soaked it in water to stop the fine ash from filling his lungs.

She finished off the knot at the back and they rejoined Nubia between two pillars of the dining room. They watched the Roman fleet move across the bay like insects crawling across a polished jade table.

Occasionally, they felt the ground vibrate and saw the tree-shaped plume of ash thicken and change colour. The air had been growing denser, and it was harder to make out details.

'Have they reached the coast?' asked Aristo anxiously.

'Bug-boats stop,' said Nubia quietly.

'Are they disembarking?' Tascius asked.

'What are they doing?' Jonathan held Pliny's sachet of herbs under his napkin and Flavia noticed he wasn't wheezing.

'I don't know . . .' said Tascius, wiping the sweat from his face with his forearm. 'Perhaps the shore is blocked. It's hard to tell. It seems to be getting dark early today.'

'It *is* dark, isn't it?' murmured Aristo.

'Look at the sun,' said Flavia. 'It's as red as blood.'

'The sun will be turned to darkness and the moon to blood at the end of this world,' said a voice behind them and they all turned to look.

Mordecai slowly pulled the linen cloth over Xanthus's face. Then he bowed his head and recited the prayer for the dead.

Lupus watched as Pliny's sailors lifted Vulcan out of the rowing boat into the warship and laid him in the cabin, on the admiral's couch.

'By the gods, he looks dreadful!' wheezed Pliny.

The smith's burns and cuts had not been washed by salt water, as Lupus's had. His face and body were terrible to see. For a long moment the admiral stood looking down at Vulcan. Then he turned to Lupus.

'He rowed all this way from Rectina's villa? Impossible!'

Lupus shrugged.

'And then when he was hit by debris from the volcano you swam the rest of the way?'

Lupus nodded and Pliny frowned. 'If I believed in the gods . . .' The admiral shook his head and opened his canvas parasol. 'Come Lupus, if you're not too tired you can help us continue our observations.'

Lupus was exhausted, but he followed the admiral and his scribe to the front of the boat. The three of them leaned over the bronze beak of the ship and

166

gazed across the water towards the volcano. Behind them the oarsmen sang their fast chant and the oars rose and fell in time.

The breeze was with them, too, and presently Lupus thought he could make out the red roof of Rectina's villa by a row of cypress trees. Was that a figure standing on the jetty? Or just a post? The ash made it hard to see.

The wind must have shifted slightly, for suddenly a shower of gravel and pieces of flaming rock rattled down onto the parasol.

'Fascinating,' murmured Pliny, and turned to his scribe. 'Phrixus, make a note of this: ashes falling hotter and thicker as we approach the shore, mixed with bits of pumice and blackened . . . um, stones, charred and cracked by the flames.' Pliny abruptly broke off in a coughing fit.

Suddenly the lookout cried, 'Shallow water and rocks ahead, admiral!'

Pliny leaned over the rail and then whirled to face the men.

'Stop!' he wheezed, holding up his hand and then, 'Back row, back row!' He collapsed into another fit of coughing.

The oarsmen deftly flipped their blades, then man-oeuvred to stop the forward movement of the ship.

Lupus saw one of the officers quickly run a pennant up a rope. It fluttered at the top of the mainmast, warning the other warships of danger.

'By the gods,' muttered Pliny as his coughing subsided. 'The shore is blocked with debris. We'll never reach them now!'

As he spoke a flaming boulder the size of a millstone hit the water less than three yards ahead of them. Its impact rocked the boat and spattered them with hot water.

'The water's hot, almost boiling!' gasped Pliny. 'Phrixus, make a note of that!'

The scribe ignored his request.

'Master!' he cried. 'Your parasol is on fire! Quickly!'

Pliny hurled the flaming parasol overboard and the three of them hurried back to the shelter of the cabin as another shower of hot gravel rained down on their heads. Once under cover, the admiral turned and peered towards the shore again.

'We can't go forward,' said Pliny. 'I see no way to get to Rectina.'

Behind them, on the admiral's couch, Vulcan groaned.

'Admiral!' cried the helmsman. 'We must turn back now. The mountain is hurling down great stones at us and the shore is completely blocked by them. if we remain here the fleet will be destroyed. We must go back!'

'No,' wheezed Pliny after a moment. 'No retreat. I shall not go back!' He thought for a moment and then snapped his fingers.

'I know what we'll do! Send the other warships

back to Misenum. They must take shelter there. I cannot afford to lose the entire imperial fleet. As for us, we will make for Tascius at Stabia, in case Rectina has been able to make her way back to him.'

Lupus grasped the admiral's arm and shook his head violently. He knew Rectina would wait for them at her villa.

'No! I've made up my mind,' announced the admiral, impatiently shaking Lupus's hand from his arm. He turned to the helmsman and said: 'The wind is behind us, we'll make excellent time. Those are your new orders: head for Stabia. "Fortune favours the brave",' he quoted. And added to Phrixus, 'You can write that down.'

'Behold!' cried Nubia. 'Bug-boats going home.'

'Are they?' cried Tascius, wiping his eyes with his hand, 'Jupiter! My eyes sting. Can't see properly. It does look as if – but the fleet hasn't had time to take on passengers.'

'Nubia's right,' said Jonathan miserably. 'They're turning back.'

'Jupiter blast it!' cursed Tascius, turning away.

'Be happy!' cried Nubia, still watching the bay. 'One bug-boat comes here!'

Lupus stood at the stern of Pliny's flagship and looked back across the water at Herculaneum, disappearing into the fog of ash behind them. The cloak drawn over his head and shoulders hardly protected him from the angry rain of hot gravel, but he did not care.

His eyes were fixed on a tiny figure in orange, where the silver-green olive trees met the water.

The ash in the air stung his eyes and made them stream, but he did not blink. He watched the figure grow smaller and smaller, until finally he could no longer see her.

SCROLL XXX

From a distance, the approaching warship had looked clean and sleek, but as it drew near, Flavia saw that it was smudged with soot and scorch marks.

She was standing between Jonathan and Nubia beneath the umbrella pines near Tascius's private jetty. The three friends and their dogs watched the oars rise and fall like the wings of a bird, then dip to slow the warship. Carried forward by its own speed, the warship slid up beside Tascius's private jetty, just nudging his private yacht.

The two slaves guarding Tascius's boat had also been sheltering under the pines. Now they ran onto the short pier, caught ropes thrown by the sailors, and tied them firmly to the docking posts.

There was a strong swell in the scummy water. The ship rose and fell as the water slapped against the jetty, making it difficult to disembark, but finally the sailors manoeuvred the boarding plank over the side. The first person off the ship was an exhausted boy in an oversized tunic.

'Lupus!' Flavia and her friends cried, and rushed forward to greet him.

Two sailors carried Vulcan's stretcher up the marble steps and into Tascius's dining-room. The smith was still unconscious, so they lifted him onto a dining couch. Miriam propped him up on the black and white silk cushions and Mordecai began to bathe his head wound with vinegar and oil.

Lupus, red-eyed with grief and exhaustion, took a long drink of water, climbed onto another couch and instantly fell asleep.

A moment later Admiral Pliny puffed up the steps behind them. He went straight to Tascius, who was staring down at the unconscious blacksmith.

'Is Rectina here?' asked Pliny. 'Has she arrived back from Herculaneum?'

Tascius looked up at him, speechless.

'She sent word for me to rescue her,' said the admiral, 'but I'm afraid there was no way we could reach her. I'm sorry, old friend. I'd hoped . . .' He stopped to catch his breath and look around.

'Flavia Gemina! You're here! And Mordecai ben Ezra, too. Excellent. You can have a look at my sailors, doctor. Many are suffering burns and cuts.' He turned back to Tascius.

'My dear Titus. May we make use of your excellent baths before dinner?'

'A bath? You want a bath?'

'If you don't mind.'

'I've very few slaves left,' stammered Tascius, 'No

one to light the furnace for hot water. There's always the cold plunge . . .'

'Excellent.' The admiral mopped his forehead. 'Just what's needed on such a hot and stifling day. Bring your tablet and stylus, Phrixus, we'll continue to take notes. Would anyone else like to accompany me?'

'Wait!' cried Jonathan, his voice slightly muffled behind his napkin. 'You can't just go and bathe as if nothing were wrong. There's a volcano erupting less than five miles away!'

'Aren't you going to rescue us?' Flavia asked.

'Sailing us away in your bug-boat?' said Nubia.

'Out of the question, I'm afraid,' wheezed the admiral. 'It's already growing dark. My men and I need to eat and by the time we've dined it will be night. I suggest we all get a good night's sleep and set off at first light tomorrow morning. It's really not too bad down here at Stabia, you know. Not compared to Herculaneum and Pompeii.'

The tree-shaped cloud which stood over the volcano was deep red in the light of the sinking sun. Jonathan, Flavia and Nubia stood watching it.

'If we had walked south along the coastal road,' Jonathan said, 'we would be miles away by now.' His voice was muffled behind his napkin.

'I think it's easing off,' said Flavia.

'What?'

Flavia lifted her own napkin away from her mouth.

'I said I think the volcano is stopping. The noise isn't as loud as it was before.'

'The floor is not shivering so much now,' said Nubia. She wore a napkin, too.

'I guess so.' Jonathan slumped against one of the columns. 'I just wish we were far away from here. I wish we were back home in Ostia.'

Flavia tried to cheer Jonathan.

'This was a good idea of yours, wearing napkins.'

After a hasty dinner of ash-coated bread and cheese, everyone had followed Jonathan's example and tied moistened napkins over nose and mouth to keep the fine ash out. Admiral Pliny, still damp from his bath, agreed that it helped his breathlessness. His sailors, playing dice on the floor, all wore napkins. Even Vulcan, eyes closed and face pale against the black silk cushions, had a cloth draped over the lower half of his face.

'That can't be a good omen,' said Jonathan, looking back into the dining-room.

A combination of the sun's horizontal rays and the fine ash created a thick red light which filled the dining-room.

'It looks as if the room is full of blood,' said Jonathan. 'And everyone looks like robbers. Robbers in a room full of blood. Or am I seeing things again?'

'You're not seeing things,' said Flavia. With napkins tied over the lower halves of their faces, they did look like masked bandits.

Flavia looked at the others. For the first time she really saw people's eyes and eyebrows. She had never noticed how pale and rumpled Pliny's eyebrows were, or how beautifully Miriam's dark ones set off her eyes. Mordecai and Jonathan had handsome brows, whereas Vulcan and Tascius each seemed to have one heavy, straight eyebrow that met above the nose.

Suddenly Flavia gasped as she had a flash of pure revelation. Taking a deep breath she turned to Pliny.

'Admiral Pliny,' she began, her heart pounding, 'what was the real reason you asked us to find Vulcan?'

SCROLL XXXI

Though the sun had not set, the red light in the dining-room had become a thick purple gloom. One of Tascius's three remaining slaves, the spotty messenger boy named Gutta, began to light the oil-lamps in the villa and the torches in the garden.

'Why did I ask you to find Vulcan?' said Pliny. 'Why do you think?'

'I think you knew he was the long-lost son of Rectina, my uncle's neighbour, and I think you hoped that we would lead Vulcan to her.'

'Very astute, my dear. You're almost right. I wasn't sure he was Rectina's long-lost son, but I suspected it.' Pliny's black eyes were bright above his napkin. 'The first time I saw him I knew he looked familiar. A few days later I realised who he reminded me of: Rectina! I felt sure he must be the kidnapped child of Rectina and Tascius. I went back to see him again but –'

'Liar!' Tascius's voice was muffled behind his cloth, but the anger in it was audible.

'What?' the admiral's eyes grew wider.

'Vulcan isn't *my* son, is he?' Tascius had risen to his feet.

'What do you mean?'

Tascius was trembling. 'He's yours!'

'I don't know what you're talking about.' Pliny sounded genuinely surprised.

'I know that you and Rectina were lovers! This *cripple* is the result of your betrayal!'

Pliny stood and pulled the napkin away from his nose and mouth.

'How dare you say such a thing? Who gave you such an idea?'

'You weren't content to steal my father's affections. You had to take those of my wife as well.'

A look of genuine dismay replaced the anger on Pliny's face. 'My dear Titus,' he said gravely. 'You are very much mistaken. Rectina and I have great affection and respect for one another, but we were never lovers.'

'Liar!' said Tascius, tearing his own cloth away from his face and throwing it onto the ground. 'This cripple is your son, not mine.' Tascius marched over to Vulcan's couch and wrenched the boot from his right foot. 'Look! Here is proof of the gods' displeasure!'

Everyone stared in horror at Vulcan's twisted foot. It was red and rounded like a clenched fist. Miriam stifled a sob and hid her face in her father's robes. On his couch, Vulcan stirred and groaned. His long eyelashes fluttered.

Mordecai stepped forward, his dark eyes angry between turban and napkin. 'You can't possibly take this as proof that he isn't your son.' He picked up the blacksmith's boot and struggled to replace it.

'But he isn't. He's not my son.'

Flavia turned towards Tascius.

'Yes he is!' she cried. 'Can't you see the resemblance between you? Look at his eyebrows! If he has Rectina's mouth and nose and eyes, well, Vulcan has your eyebrows!'

'Eyebrows!' snorted Tascius. 'Eyebrows, indeed!'

'She's right, father.' Vulcan opened his eyes. 'Mother told me the truth. I am your son, your only son, whom you abandoned.'

Admiral Pliny stared at Tascius. 'You? *You* are the one who abandoned him?'

Tascius hung his head.

'You abandoned him because you thought he was mine?'

Tascius nodded.

'Do you realise what you've done?' said Pliny. 'You abandoned your own child, lived a lie for seventeen years, and ultimately drove your wife and daughters away, probably to their deaths.'

Tascius lifted his head and stared at Pliny stupidly, like a boxer who has received too many blows.

'Rectina never loved anyone but you,' said Pliny steadily. 'She was always faithful to you, just as a Roman matron should be.' He gestured towards Vulcan. 'And this young man . . . Titus. Listen to me. This is one of the most courageous young men I have ever known. He is your son, Titus, your own flesh and blood. And you should be proud of him. As proud of him as your own father was of you.'

Everyone stared at Tascius as he slowly turned to look at Vulcan. In the flickering lamplight his eyes were shadowed.

'Is it true?' he said. 'Are you . . . ?'

Vulcan turned his head away and closed his eyes. He was weeping. To the north the volcano rumbled ominously.

Tascius took a faltering step towards the couch.

'Vulcan?'

The grey-haired soldier stood over the dining couch and took the young man's battered hands in his own. He studied them, then kissed them gently and pressed them to his face. His shoulders shook and soon Vulcan's hands were wet with his father's tears.

Presently, Tascius pulled the signet ring from the third finger of his hand and held it up for all to see.

'Great Jove!' he began, but his voice broke and he had to start again. 'Great Jove! I declare in front of all these witnesses that this young man is my true son and heir.' He gently pushed the ring onto the little finger of Vulcan's left hand. 'From this moment on, all that I have is his, and he shall no longer be known as Vulcan, but by his given name: Publius Tascius Pomponianus.'

*

'I can't think of him as "Publius",' whispered Flavia to Jonathan and Nubia. 'He'll always be Vulcan.'

'I know,' agreed Jonathan, and Nubia nodded, too.

It was long past sundown and outside it was pitch black, except for where the torches burned.

Admiral Pliny had gone to bed, but none of the rest of them could sleep. No one wanted to be far from the lamplight, and no one wanted to be alone.

Gutta was sweeping ash from the floor and some of Pliny's sailors were still playing dice at a low table.

Tascius had pulled a chair up beside his son's couch and for a long time the two of them had been deep in quiet conversation. Every so often Tascius raised a cup of well-watered wine to the young man's lips and helped him to drink. Sometimes they wept together. Presently they called Mordecai over and Flavia heard the three men discussing the meaning of the donkey riddle.

She approached them almost shyly.

Vulcan looked up at her and smiled.

'Hello, Flavia Gemina,' he said. 'I must thank you.'

'For what?' said Flavia. 'I didn't think about your feelings. All I cared about was the treasure.'

'I don't believe you,' smiled the blacksmith. 'I think you are a girl who seeks the truth. And your desire for knowledge helped me find my parents: my mother . . .' he swallowed, 'and my father.'

Tascius gripped his son's hand so hard that the knuckles grew white.

'How can I thank you?' whispered the young man.

'Will you tell me what the riddle really means, and what the treasure is?'

SCROLL XXXII

Lupus had finally woken from his deep sleep. Although the night was stifling and hot, he pulled a linen cover round his shoulders and came to sit with Flavia, Jonathan, and Nubia on the floor beside Vulcan's couch.

'So. You want to know the meaning of the riddle and what the treasure is?' The young blacksmith tried to sit forward and then sank back weakly against his cushions.

'Careful, Publius,' said Tascius, and patted his son's shoulder.

'I think I know what some of it means,' said Flavia. 'I think "jackass" is a password for Christians, because you worship the donkey.'

There was a pause. Then Jonathan yelped, 'What?'

'I saw you worshipping the donkey in the stables,' explained Flavia.

'We don't worship a donkey!' Jonathan cried. 'Our God is invisible.'

'Oh,' said Flavia.

'But you were right to think it's a password,' said Vulcan. 'Our faith is illegal so we must be careful. The donkey is just one of many codewords, which show us aspects of our God.'

'So your invisible God is a bit like a shepherd and a bit like a donkey?' said Flavia.

'And he's a bit like a dolphin and an anchor and an eagle and a warrior,' said Jonathan. 'That's my favourite: the warrior.'

'But how is he like a jackass?'

'You tell me,' said Vulcan.

'Gentle and patient and humble?'

'Exactly.'

'And with big ears and soft fur?' said Nubia gravely. Then she giggled.

'Hey! Nubia's first joke!' cried Jonathan, and slapped the African girl on the back.

Vulcan smiled, too. 'Also, each letter of the word jackass – *ASINE* – has another deeper meaning. If you study them, the letters show you how to journey along the Way.'

'What way?'

'The Way to joy and fulfilment in this life, and Paradise in the next.'

'That's the treasure beyond imagining?' said Flavia.

Vulcan nodded.

'So it's not *real* treasure?' She couldn't help feeling disappointed.

'Of course it is, Flavia!' said Vulcan. 'You of all people should know that sometimes the greatest treasure is knowledge. Knowing how to meet with

God.' He looked at his father. 'Knowing how to forgive. Knowing how to find joy in a world of pain, and afterwards the greatest treasure of all. Eternal life. Not in a dark and shadowy underworld, but in a green and sunny Paradise, reunited with those we love. What treasure could be better than that?'

Behind them, Miriam had begun to weep.

Vulcan looked at her with concern.

'She's worried about Uncle Gaius,' explained Flavia.

'Where is he?'

'He went to Pompeii and Oplontis to warn the inhabitants about the volcano, remember?' said Flavia.

'And he isn't back yet?'

Flavia shook her head.

'It's dark now,' said Nubia. 'Miriam worried that dark.'

Vulcan nodded, and looked at Miriam for a long time.

'And you're worried about Clio, aren't you?' said Jonathan to Lupus.

Lupus nodded.

They were all silent for a few minutes. Then Nubia reached out and touched the finger on which Lupus usually wore his ring: 'Give wolf-ring to Clio?' she asked.

Lupus nodded again.

Suddenly, Tigris whimpered and emerged from beneath a couch where he'd been sheltering with

Scuto and Nipur. He padded to the steps and sniffed the murky air.

'What is it, boy?' asked Jonathan, getting to his feet and following him. 'What do you see out there?'

The others peered out into the darkness towards the volcano.

Then they saw it too.

Moving straight towards them out of the ash-black night, illuminated by the torches on the lawn, were two gleaming yellow eyes: the eyes of a wounded beast.

Tigris barked and wagged his small tail, but the rest of them stood frozen as the creature moved into the torchlight.

'Ferox!' cried Jonathan. 'It's Ferox!'

From the other side of the room, Miriam gave a cry and ran to the step that led down into darkness. Then she screamed.

Ferox was bloody and wounded. One ear was torn from his head and his left rear leg hung useless. The foam round his muzzle was flecked with blood and his breath came in wheezing gasps. He looked up at them and whined.

'Master of the Universe!' whispered Mordecai and cautiously stepped forward to examine the wounded dog. Ferox whined again and wagged his tail feebly. As Mordecai reached out a hand to touch the matted fur on the dog's chest, Ferox growled softly and flinched.

Mordecai looked down at his fingertips. They were smeared with blood.

'These wounds were inflicted by man and not by volcanic rock,' said Mordecai grimly.

'He must have been protecting Gaius!' cried Miriam. She clutched her father's arm.

Ferox turned as if to go back into the night, then looked over his shoulder at them and whined imploringly.

'Ferox want to follow,' said Nubia, turning her amber eyes on Flavia and Jonathan.

'No way I'm going out there,' muttered Jonathan.

'Uncle Gaius out there maybe,' suggested Nubia.

'Gaius?' cried Miriam. 'Out there? Then I'm going to follow Ferox!' She hurried down the steps onto the ash-covered lawn and wrenched one of the garden torches from its holder. Then she turned to look back up at them. With the yellow flames flickering on her black curls, and all but her eyes hidden by a cloth, she looked like a beautiful bandit.

'I'll come with you,' said Tascius. 'It's time I showed half the courage you all have.'

'We'll come, too!' offered two of the sailors. They were gazing at Miriam in awe, and as she moved off into the swirling ash they hurried after her.

Flavia and her friends looked at each other. Without a word they hurried down the steps, grasped torches and followed the others into the night.

*

As they followed the wounded animal into the darkness, the globes of light from their pine torches lit the falling ash. It floated down around them like warm black snow, muffling every sound except for the constant thunder of the volcano.

Chest deep in ash, Ferox limped ahead, his left hind leg dangling uselessly. Occasionally he would stop and utter a soft whine, looking back to make sure they were still following. Nubia whispered words of encouragement in her own language. They followed him across the ash-covered lawn, through the open gate and up the drive.

Presently, they could hear the noise of pack animals and carriage wheels and see the dim globes of torch-light through the ash. They were approaching the coastal road. A steady stream of refugees were making their way along it towards the south.

They found his body at the roadside shrine of Mercury. It was already covered with two inches of ash. Ferox nosed the still form of his master and whined up at them pitifully. Miriam cried out and ran forward. One of the sailors took her torch as she knelt and brushed away the ash.

'Gaius!' she cried, 'Gaius, my love. Speak to me. Tell me you're still alive!'

She pulled back the cloak from his head. Gaius's face was cut and bleeding. His nose had been broken and there was an ugly knife wound across his left cheekbone. One eye was swollen shut but the other flickered and then opened. As he looked up at Miriam, one corner of his mouth pulled up in what looked to Flavia like a grimace.

But she knew it was a smile.

SCROLL XXXIII

'I don't know if he'll live,' said Mordecai gravely. 'The stab wound in his chest pierced a lung. His leg is broken and he has been badly beaten. He is also suffering from a number of dog bites.'

'But you have to save him, father,' cried Miriam. 'He saved Gaius's life. Without him Gaius would be dead now, buried by ash!'

They were back in Tascius's dining-room. Mordecai knelt on a blanket spread on the floor and examined Ferox. Jonathan assisted his father.

Flavia's uncle Gaius lay on a couch nearby. He had eaten some bread and cheese and had drained a jug of diluted wine. Now Miriam was gently sponging his cuts and wounds with a vinegar-soaked sea-sponge.

'He saved my life . . .' Gaius's lip was swollen where he had been hit. 'Four of them and a huge mastiff. Wanted the horse. Ferox killed the mastiff and wounded two of the men. Couldn't fight other two off. They beat me. Took horse.' He closed his eyes from the effort and Miriam put her cool finger gently on his battered lips.

'Shhh! Don't speak, my love,' she said. 'Father will do everything he can to save him.'

When Mordecai finished dressing Ferox's wounds he got to his feet. 'The only thing we can do now is pray.'

Ferox lay on the blanket, panting. He rolled his eyes up at the doctor and then over towards Gaius. He whined softly.

'Yes,' said Mordecai quietly. 'He's alive. You saved him. Good dog.' As he spoke, Jonathan bent and placed something in the folds of the blanket, then stepped back. Tail wagging, Tigris sniffed Ferox. Then the puppy licked the big dog's face and curled up beside him. Ferox lowered his big head, uttered a deep sigh, and slept.

It was after midnight when the mountain exploded. None of them were really sleeping, apart from Pliny, whose snores could be heard by those making their way to or from the latrine. The rest dozed in the dining-room or talked quietly together, waiting for the dawn.

Suddenly a brilliant orange flash lit the room and a moment later the whole house trembled under a deafening wave of sound. Everyone looked at the growing column of fire which rose slowly up from the mountain. In its light they could see that the top of Vesuvius was completely gone.

'Jupiter,' muttered Tascius. 'It's getting worse.'

Another quake shook the house and Flavia actually saw the columns sway back and forth. Some of the lamps fell to the floor and shattered, spilling hot oil. A snake of fire slipped from one shattered clay lamp, writhed across the floor and down the steps, then died.

Jonathan staggered into the room from the direction of the latrines.

'Come quickly,' he cried, his voice muffled behind his cloth. 'Pliny's door is blocked. He'll be trapped!'

Mordecai, Tascius and a dozen of Pliny's sailors hurried after Jonathan. Flavia and Nubia followed.

No one had swept the courtyard and it had quickly filled up with ash and bits of pumice stone. The level of the debris was almost up to Flavia's knees. The sailors tried to wade through the grey ash, cursing as they went.

'It's hardening,' said one of them.

'Like cement,' confirmed the other.

They tried to open the wooden door of the bedroom, but it wouldn't budge.

'He must be terrified!' cried Flavia. 'He's probably been crying out for hours.'

One of the sailors put his ear to the door and the other one pressed his forefinger to his lips. But there was no need. From right across the courtyard and even above the rumble of the volcano, they could all hear the admiral snoring.

After nearly half an hour, the sailors had chipped away

enough of the hardened ash to open Pliny's door. The tapping had woken Phrixus, who helped by pushing the door from inside. At last he was able to help his master through the narrow opening and into the ash-filled courtyard.

'What do you want?' grumbled Pliny irritably. 'Why have you woken me?'

'Well, apart from the fact that the mountain is melting like wax, the house is falling down around us and you were about to be buried alive, no reason,' muttered Jonathan.

'Haven't you felt any of the quakes?' cried Tascius. He helped his friend into the dining-room. 'And don't you see those sheets of fire flaring up on Vesuvius?'

The admiral peered through the columns towards the mountain.

'Bonfires,' he announced after a moment.

'Bonfires?' echoed Mordecai.

'Yes,' the admiral wheezed. 'No doubt they flared up when cowardly peasants left their homes in a hurry and their hearths caught fire.'

A huge flash lit the sky, silhouetting the decapitated cone of Vesuvius for an instant.

'And that?' asked Aristo.

'An empty house catching fire, from the sparks showering down upon it. Nothing to worry about. Let me go back to sleep and wake me at dawn.'

There was another explosion and again the sky was

lurid red for a long moment. Far away they could hear people screaming.

'See,' gestured Pliny. 'Cowardly peasants. Nothing to worry about, I say. Back to bed . . .'

Abruptly, the whole house seemed to rock on its foundations. From somewhere nearby there was an enormous crash and a scream.

Gutta the slave-boy hurried in. 'The roof of the baths has just caved in!'

'Anyone hurt?' asked Tascius in alarm.

'No,' said the slave, and fainted.

'We must get out of here before the whole house comes down around our heads,' said Mordecai, passing a tiny bottle beneath Gutta's nose.

'But you're tending the ill and wounded,' wheezed Pliny, gesturing at Gaius and Vulcan on their couches. 'How can they travel?'

'We could take Vulcan's donkey,' suggested Flavia. 'And your sailors could help, too.'

'Yes, very well,' said Pliny, staggering to remain upright as another quake shook the house. 'I suppose we could go down to the beach and see if it's possible to make our escape by ship.' He glared at the volcano. 'It does appear to be getting a little worse.'

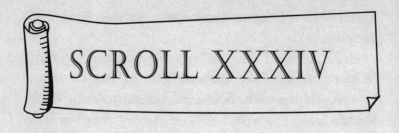

'Miriam, your hair is on fire!' screamed Flavia Gemina.

They had just set out for the beach when a shower of flaming pumice stones rained down upon them and Miriam's dark hair burst into flame.

Before Miriam could panic or run, her father had enveloped her head with his robes, smothering the flames.

'Father, it hurts,' Miriam sobbed, and Mordecai pulled her back up the steps into the dining-room. Everyone followed.

'See?' gasped the admiral. 'It's death out there. We'd do much better to remain here.'

'No,' said Mordecai. 'We must go, or I'll lose both my children.' He nodded at Jonathan, who was pale and wheezing. 'Can't you smell it?' said Mordecai. 'It's sulphur.'

'I know what we can do,' gasped Jonathan. 'Cushions! We'll tie cushions . . . to our heads. To keep off . . . the burning pumice.'

Pliny gazed at him for a moment. 'You really are the most resourceful children. Unless anyone has a better idea, I suggest we take young Jonathan's advice!'

With a striped silk cushion tied to his head and two across his back, Scuto led the way down to the shore.

Earlier, the fall of ash had been like silent black snow, now it was fiery rain. The volcano's rumble was deeper, angrier now, and flashes of lightning flickered ominously above its cone. Despite the muffling ash, they could hear women and children screaming and men crying out.

With cushions tied to their heads and the damp napkins still knotted to cover their noses and mouths, they made their way through the blackness down towards Tascius's jetty.

Flavia could see a line of torches extending ahead of her. There were at least fifty of them. Forty of Pliny's sailors headed the procession, followed by the admiral and Phrixus. Gaius rode the donkey, with Miriam and Mordecai walking either side of him. The sailors had chopped up the dining-room couches to make two stretchers. They carried Vulcan on one, Ferox on the other.

Nubia had showed Jonathan how to make slings for the puppies, like the ones the women in her clan made for their babies. Behind them stumbled Flavia and Lupus, flanking Aristo, who carried old Frustilla on his back. Taking up the rear was the slave-boy Gutta.

Most of them held a torch or lamp. Even so, it was darker than any night Flavia had ever known. Presently, the torches at the front slowed and stopped. Something was happening up ahead.

'What is it?' Flavia called out, then adjusted her cushion as a shower of sparks fell on her.

'Too rough,' came the reply from Mordecai, relaying what he'd heard Pliny say. 'The sea is still too rough for sailing. There is no escape that way. We must go along the beach towards Stabia.'

Flavia had never been so tired. She tried to concentrate on just placing one foot in front of the other. She prayed to Castor and Pollux, and she prayed to Vulcan – the god of volcanoes – and not for the first time she prayed to the Shepherd. She prayed that she and her friends might live.

Earlier in the evening she had felt hopeful. It seemed as if the volcano was not going to be the disaster they had all feared.

Now she felt only despair. The sun should have risen by now, but it was darker than ever, and all her hope had been quenched by oppressive heat, darkness and exhaustion. She wished she had slept earlier, for now she could barely keep her eyes open.

The refugees had turned on their heels, so that now Gutta and Flavia led the way down along the beach while Pliny and his sailors took up the rear. It seemed as if they had been walking for hours.

There was another awful roar from the mountain behind them and everyone turned wearily to see what new terror the gods had dreamed up.

Although they were miles from Vesuvius, they all clearly saw what happened next.

Of all the horrors the volcano had produced so far, this was the worst.

As when soda is added to wine vinegar and it bubbles and froths over the edge of the cup, so a tide of fire poured down the volcano's cone. This was not a drift of warm ash falling gently from the heavens or a slow lava flow. This was a wave of yellow fire rushing towards them faster than galloping horses. The speeding flames lit up distant houses and olive groves and vineyards, and left them blazing as it passed.

Flavia saw a row of tall poplar trees explode and then burn like torches. The poplars were two or three miles distant but already the ring of fire was bearing down upon them.

'Down!' bellowed Tascius, in his commander's voice. 'Get down on the sand.'

Aristo had already eased Frustilla off his back. Now he pushed Flavia and Nubia face down onto the sand. Flavia's cushion slipped halfway off her head. She had just pushed it back in place when the wave was upon them. A roaring heat, almost unbearable, made her ears pop and sucked the air from her lungs. Then it had passed.

Hesitantly, Flavia opened her eyes. And cried out. She was blind.

SCROLL XXXV

Men were screaming, crying to the gods for mercy or help. In her blindness, Flavia heard one of Pliny's big sailors cry out for his mother. Another shrieked, 'Let me die!' over and over.

Then a light flickered and flared and illuminated Aristo's wonderful face.

Flavia sobbed with relief. She wasn't blind. The blast of hot air had extinguished all the torches. Aristo had used a sulphur stick to rekindle his.

Soon they had all lit their torches and lamps from his one flame, and they could see each other again.

Some of the sailors hadn't been prompt in following Tascius's order. The wave of fire had knocked them to the ground, scorching their eyebrows and reddening their faces as if they'd been burnt by the sun.

'We're five miles from the mountain,' breathed Aristo, picking up Frustilla and dusting her off. 'What must that have been like for those at its foot?'

'Or those on the water,' said Mordecai grimly. His beard was singed and the locks of hair that hung from his turban burnt right away. 'It was a mercy we were not able to board the ship after all.'

'No one near Vesuvius could have survived that,' said Flavia, then bit her lip as she saw the look on Lupus's face. Tascius stared bleakly at the mountain, too. If Rectina and her daughters had remained at Herculaneum . . .

As they turned to move south again, Flavia was aware of something holding her back. Nubia had gripped her cloak.

'Wait,' Nubia said.

Flavia looked wearily at her slave-girl, then beyond her.

Something was happening. A group of people had stopped further back along the beach.

'What?' groaned Flavia. 'What is it?'

'I think it is the old man,' said Nubia, pointing. 'The Pliny.'

The glow of several torches marked a group of figures huddled on the sand.

'Please, master.' They heard Phrixus's voice, exhausted but urgent.

Flavia turned and stumbled back towards the group on the beach. She hadn't even the strength to ask the others to wait.

The wave of fire seemed to have purified the air and for a moment she imagined it was easier to breathe. She could see the group clearly in the flickering torchlight. Someone had spread a sailcloth on the beach and the admiral was sitting on it. Phrixus knelt beside him, and as she came closer Flavia saw the slave's handsome face, smudged with soot and twisted in concern for his master. Three big sailors stood over their admiral, holding their torches and looking down helplessly.

Further back on the shore, a spark had ignited the sail of a beached ship. As the timbers caught fire it began to burn fiercely. The flames gave off a bright yellow light and illuminated the group on the sand.

Flavia sank onto the sailcloth beside Pliny and touched his shoulder. The old man lifted his head and gave her a feeble smile. The dark cushion on his head gave him an almost jaunty look. He had pulled the napkin away from his face and was breathing into the small sachet which hung from his neck. It was similar to the one he had given Jonathan, filled with herbs to bring relief for breathlessness.

Flavia suddenly felt her heart would break. What good would a little herb pouch do in this nightmare of ash, sparks and noxious gases?

The admiral tried to snap his fingers and both Phrixus and Flavia leaned nearer.

'What do you want, master?' asked Phrixus. Tears streaked the soot on his cheeks.

'Your wax tablets and stylus?' Flavia suggested.

Pliny gave another feeble smile and shook his head. His lips moved. Flavia and Phrixus both brought their ears closer. Flavia couldn't make out his words, but Phrixus understood.

'Water. He wants a little cold water . . .'

The scribe stood up and looked around desperately.

'Water!' he cried. 'Does anyone have water?'

Everyone shook their heads. Few had thought to bring water, though they would have given anything for a mouthful to wash away the ashes from their mouths. For ashes were the taste of death. Flavia suddenly saw from Pliny's face that he tasted his own death. Phrixus saw it, too.

'Water. Please bring him water!'

A short figure moved out of the gloom and knelt beside the admiral. It was Gutta, the spotty slave from Tascius's villa. He uncorked a gourd and poured a stream of water into the admiral's thirsty mouth.

Pliny gripped the boy's wrist and drank the water greedily. At last he nodded his thanks to the slave and curled up on the canvas sheet. Flavia heard his voice, stronger now, but still barely audible. 'A little nap. That's all I need. Just a little nap.'

Suddenly the smell of rotten eggs hit the back of Flavia's throat and almost made her gag. She knew they must get away from the deadly fumes, or die.

'Sulphur!' cried Tascius, looming out of the darkness. 'We must go quickly, before we are overcome! Come on, old friend.'

Phrixus and Gutta helped the admiral to his feet. Pliny stood leaning on the two young slaves. The pillow tied to his head had slipped to one side.

'We must go, master,' cried Phrixus. 'The sulphur.'

The curtain of ash parted for a moment and they could all see the admiral, lit by the red and yellow flames of the burning boat.

Pliny gazed back at them and tried to say something. Then he collapsed, like a child's rag doll, into the arms of Phrixus and Gutta. They eased him back onto the sailcloth.

Mordecai was at his side in an instant. He loosened the admiral's clothing and pressed two fingers against the side of Pliny's neck. After a moment he put his ear to the admiral's mouth. Finally he looked up at them and slowly shook his head.

Pliny was dead.

SCROLL XXXVI

They left the admiral's body there on the shore.

The sulphur fumes were still choking. Jonathan and Frustilla were both struggling for breath. One of the big Roman oarsmen took the old cook onto his back and jogged ahead, another carried Jonathan. Their fellow-sailors lit the way. Someone said the promontory was not far off. If they could get round it, the air might be clearer.

It was their only hope of survival.

To Flavia, dazed with exhaustion, everything was vague after that. They left the beach and made their way up to the coast road where the going was a little easier. Once round the promontory they found that the sulphur fumes were not as powerful, and the fall of ash was much lighter.

Beside a small cove was a seaside tavern with a boathouse attached. Many people were sheltering there, under the large brick vaults. They found a spot on the far wall and huddled against a rolled-up fishing net. Flavia was dimly aware of the faithful donkey Modestus standing patiently nearby. Then someone doused all the torches but one and she fell into a fitful sleep.

After a long time, Nubia shook Flavia awake. The tavern-keeper was bringing water round to the refugees. The small flame of his clay lamp illuminated the blackness around them.

Flavia waited for Nubia, then she took the clay beaker and drank. The water was cold and fizzy and smelled of eggs, but it washed the taste of death from her mouth. Vaguely, as if in a dream, she heard Mordecai's accented voice.

'How much is the water? I have gold.'

'Nothing. No charge,' said the innkeeper.

'But why?'

'The Master says: If you give even a cup of cold water, you will not lose your reward . . .'

Flavia drifted off into sleep again.

She dreamt of magpies carrying Rectina and her daughters up into the heavens.

She dreamt of Pliny, sailing away on a wax tablet with a sheet of papyrus for his sail. In her dream he turned back and waved at her cheerfully as he sailed towards a blue horizon.

She dreamt of Ferox playing with Scuto and the puppies in her sunny garden back home in Ostia.

She dreamt of a baby, with Miriam's dark curls and Gaius's grey eyes.

Finally she dreamt of Vulcan. He stood at his forge, his torso gleaming and polished as bronze. He looked happy. His burns and cuts had healed and both his feet were whole. He was forging armour for Achilles, the warrior son of Thetis. Then Achilles – golden Achilles – stepped into the darkness of the smithy. Vulcan handed him the armour of light and the warrior put it on.

Achilles turned to look at Flavia, who was now also in the dream. He smiled at her. Suddenly he was too bright to look at. Flavia squinted and tried to see his face. Dressed in his armour, he shone like the sun. Then she saw that he was the sun.

The endless night had ended and day had come again.

'Behold!' said a soft voice beside her. 'The sun.'

Flavia nodded and squeezed Nubia's hand.

They had survived the volcano.

FINIS

ARISTO'S SCROLL

Achilles (uh-*kill*-ease)
   Greek hero of the Trojan war and son of the sea-nymph
   Thetis
amphora (am-*for*-a)
   large clay storage jar for holding wine, oil or grain
atrium (*eh*-tree-um)
   the reception room in larger Roman homes, often with
   skylight and rainwater pool
capsa (*cap*-sa)
   cylindrical leather case, usually for medical implements
carruca (ca-*roo*-ka)
   a four-wheeled travelling coach, often covered
Castor and Pollux
   the famous Twins of Greek mythology, special guardians
   of sailors and of the Geminus family
Catullus (cuh-*tull*-us)
   Latin poet famous for his love poems
ceramic (sir-*am*-ik)
   clay which has been fired in a kiln, very hard and
   smooth
cicada (sick-*eh*-dah)
   an insect like a grasshopper that chirrs during the day

en (en)

Latin word meaning 'behold!' or 'look!'

Flavia (*flay*-vee-a)

a name, meaning 'fair-haired'; Flavius is the masculine form of this name

forum (*for*-um)

ancient marketplace and civic centre in Roman towns

freedman (*freed*-man)

a slave who has been granted freedom

garland (*gar*-land)

a wreath of flowers entwined with ivy worn at dinner parties

Gemina (*gem*-in-a)

a name, meaning 'twin'; Geminus and Gemini are other forms

Herculaneum (Herk-you-*lane*-ee-um)

the 'town of Hercules' at the foot of Vesuvius northwest of Pompeii. It was buried by mud in the eruption of AD 79

hours

the Romans counted the hours of the day from dawn. In summer, when dawn was about six o'clock, the fifth hour of the day would be 11.00 a.m. and the eleventh hour of the day around 5.00 in the afternoon

Ides (eyedz)

The Ides were one of the three key dates in the Roman calender. In most months (including August) the Ides fall on the 13th. In March, July, October and May they occur on the 15th of the month

Juno (*jew*-no)
: queen of the Roman gods and wife of the god Jupiter

Laurentum (lore-*ent*-um)
: a small town on the coast of Italy a few miles south of Ostia

Lupus (*loo*-puss)
: a Roman name; means 'wolf' in Latin

Misenum (my-*see*-num)
: Rome's chief naval harbour, near the great port of Puteoli to the north of the bay of Naples

Mordecai (*mord*-ak-eye)
: a Hebrew name

Neapolis (nay-*ap*-o-liss)
: a large city in the south of Italy, dominating a vast bay and lying at the foot of mount Vesuvius; modern Naples

Ostia (*oss*-tee-ah)
: the port of ancient Rome and home town of Flavia Gemina

palaestra (pal-*eye*-stra)
: the (usually open air) exercise area of public baths

papyrus (pa-*pie*-rus)
: the cheapest writing material, made of Egyptian reeds

pax (packs)
: Latin word meaning 'peace'

peristyle (*pare*-ee-style)
: a columned walkway around an inner garden or courtyard

Pliny (*plin*-ee)

famous Roman nobleman, an admiral and author (full name Gaius Plinius Secundus)

Pompeii (pom-*pay*)

a prosperous coastal town south of Rome on the bay of Neapolis buried by the eruption of AD 79

Puteoli (poo-tee-*oh*-lee)

the great commercial port on the bay of Naples

salve! (*sal*-vay)

Latin for 'hello!'

scroll (skrole)

a papyrus or parchment 'book', unrolled from side to side (not top to bottom) as it was read. Some books were so long that they had to be divided into several scrolls. Pliny's *Natural History* was 37 scrolls long

sestercii (sess-*tur*-see)

more than one sestercius, a silver coin

signet ring (*sig*-net ring)

ring with an image carved in it used as a personal seal, it would be pressed into soft or hot wax

Stabia (sta-*bee*-ah)

also known as Stabiae; a town to the south of Pompeii (modern Castellammare di Stabia)

stola (*stole*-a)

a girl's or woman's dress

stylus (*stile*-us)

a metal, wood or ivory tool for writing on wax tablets

tablinum (ta-*blee*-num)

a room in the Roman house, like a study

Thetis (*Thet*-iss)
    a beautiful sea-nymph who was the mother of Achilles
    and foster mother of Vulcan

toga (*toe*-ga)
    a blanket-like outer garment, worn by men and boys

triclinium (tri-*clin*-ee-um)
    the ancient Roman dining-room, so called because it
    usually had three dining couches on which the adults
    reclined to eat

tunic (*tew*-nick)
    a piece of clothing like a big T-shirt. Boys and girls
    sometimes wore a long-sleeved one

Tyrrhenian (tur-*reen*-ee-un)
    The name of the sea off the west coast of Italy

Vespasian (vess-*pay*-zhun)
    Roman Emperor who died just before this story begins
    (full name Titus Flavius Vespasianus)

Vesuvius (vuh-*soo*-vee-yus)
    a mountain near Naples, not known to be a volcano
    until it first erupted on 24 August AD 79

Vinalia (vee-*nal*-yah)
    the late summer wine festival, sacred to Venus, held
    every August 19th

Vulcan (*vul*-can)
    the blacksmith god, son of Jupiter and Juno and
    husband of Venus

Vulcanalia (vul-can-*ale*-yah)
    the two-day festival of Vulcan, held every August 23rd
    and 24th

wax tablet
> a wax-covered rectangle of wood; when the wax was
> scraped away, the wood beneath showed as a mark

THE LAST SCROLL

Vesuvius is one of the most famous volcanoes in the world. But until it erupted in August AD 79, nobody suspected it was a volcano. We know about it from two sources.

First, we have archaeological evidence: the famous 'buried cities' at the foot of the volcano. Their remains give us a glimpse of a single day in the Roman empire.

Second, we have written evidence: two letters by Pliny's young nephew, who was staying with his uncle at Misenum when the volcano erupted.

Theories about the timing of the volcano are constantly being revised, but recent studies indicate that most people survived the first twelve hours of the eruption. It was only after midnight that a series of pyroclastic flows killed those closest to the volcano.

Admiral Pliny was a real person, as were Tascius and Rectina. Vulcan, Clio, and Phrixus were not real people. But they *could* have been.

Vulcan's riddle is also real. No one knows exactly what it means.

The Roman Mysteries

THE THIEVES OF OSTIA

Flavia Gemina makes three new friends – Jonathan, Lupus and Nubia – and together they solve the mystery of why the watchdogs of Ostia are being killed. Whoever is doing it must have reason to silence them.

THE PIRATES OF POMPEII

The four friends discover that children are being kidnapped from the camps where the refugees from Pompeii shelter after the eruption of Vesuvius – and proceed to solve the mystery of the pirates of Pompeii.

THE ASSASSINS OF ROME

Jonathan disappears and his three friends trace him to the Golden House of the Emperor Nero in Rome, where they face a deadly assassin. This is the darkest mystery yet as they learn what happened to Jonathan's family in Jerusalem.

THE DOLPHINS OF LAURENTUM

Just off the coast of Laurentum, in Ostia, is a sunken wreck full of treasure. Flavia and her three friends are determined to retrieve it – but so is someone else. An exciting adventure which reveals the secret of Lupus's past.

THE TWELVE TASKS OF FLAVIA GEMINA

It's December and time for Saturnalia – the pagan festival where anything goes. There's a lion on the loose in Ostia, a mysterious woman appears, and Flavia and her friends undertake an investigation.